"Luke? Are you leaving so soon?"

Luke nodded without looking at Sara. "I have another job I need to take care of. I'll be back tomorrow."

Would he? Working with Sara had taken a new turn. Maybe he should back out of this job. It was too risky.

"Oh, all right. I'll see you then. Thanks for the help."

He cringed at the curiosity in her voice. "Did you…delete that picture you took?"

"Yes. I said I did. Why?"

He should have left well enough alone. "Just checking." He picked up the toolbox and made a beeline for the back door. "See you later."

He walked briskly toward his truck, climbed in and closed the door. What was he going to do now? What if she got curious and started probing?

Luke ran a hand down the back of his neck. He'd learned two important things about Sara Holden. She was curious and she hated secrets.

And that was a dangerous combination… because he was a man with secrets.

Lorraine Beatty was raised in Columbus, Ohio, but now calls Mississippi home. She and her husband, Joe, have two sons and five grandchildren. Lorraine started writing in junior high and is a member of RWA and ACFW and is a charter member and past president of Magnolia State Romance Writers. In her spare time she likes to work in her garden, travel and spend time with her family.

Books by Lorraine Beatty

Love Inspired

The Orphans' Blessing
Her Secret Hope
The Family He Needs
The Loner's Secret Past

Mississippi Hearts

Her Fresh Start Family
Their Family Legacy
Their Family Blessing

Home to Dover

Protecting the Widow's Heart
His Small-Town Family
Bachelor to the Rescue
Her Christmas Hero
The Nanny's Secret Child
A Mom for Christmas
The Lawman's Secret Son
Her Handyman Hero

Visit the Author Profile page at LoveInspired.com for more titles.

The Loner's Secret Past

Lorraine Beatty

LOVE INSPIRED
INSPIRATIONAL ROMANCE

LOVE INSPIRED®

INSPIRATIONAL ROMANCE

PLEASE RECYCLE
THIS PRODUCT IS RECYCLABLE

Recycling programs for this product may not exist in your area.

ISBN-13: 978-1-335-58625-4

The Loner's Secret Past

Love Inspired
22 Adelaide St. West, 41st Floor
Toronto, Ontario M5H 4E3, Canada
www.LoveInspired.com

Printed in U.S.A.

And we know that all things work together
for good to them that love God, to them
who are the called according to his purpose.
—*Romans* 8:28

For Tina, whose love, devotion and compassion helped us all through a very difficult loss. You were our rock and we are eternally grateful. Love you, Sis.

Chapter One

"What have I gotten myself into?"

Sara Holden's spirits sank as she scanned the interior of The New Again Emporium, her sister's antiques and collectibles store in Blessing, Mississippi. She'd agreed to help Camille revitalize her store and have it reopened in time for the town's Bicentennial Arts and Crafts Festival next month. However, she was now having serious doubts about keeping her promise. The store was much larger than she'd expected and cluttered with merchandise.

Sara had envisioned a cute little shop that she'd decorate quickly, then concentrate on finding a new job back in the city. She'd estimated two weeks to get the shop reorganized and opened but obviously that was unrealistic, which meant she could be stuck in this small town far longer than she wanted.

Her cell buzzed, and she pulled it from her pocket. "Hey, sis."

"Well, what do you think of my shop? I wish I could've come with you to show you around, but I have to rest."

"It's okay. Don't worry." Her sister was eight months pregnant with twins and having complications that forced her to close her store. "Your shop is much bigger than I expected."

"I know. Isn't that great? It used to be an old five-and-dime. Do you have some wonderful ideas already?"

Sara bit her lip. She had ideas all right. The idea to turn around and go back to Chicago even without a job. "I just got here, sis. But I'm going to take some measurements and look around. I'm sure I'll have some thoughts when I get back to the house."

Cammy giggled. "Oh, I just know you're going to make it charming and adorable, and everyone will want to come to my store. I'll have supper ready when you get here."

"You're supposed to be resting."

"I am but I can still fix a meal. I'll get Rusty and Jonah to help me."

Her sister had a nine year old son the same age as Sara's son, Jonah. The cousins had hit it off from the first meeting. "Where are the boys?"

"Fishing at the pond."

Sara's heart pinched. Fishing wasn't a skill she'd envisioned for her son. Jonah was her whole world, and she had vowed to give him every benefit possible. A life he couldn't get in Blessing. They were only here out of necessity. When Sara's job had been eliminated, she'd tried to hold on while looking for another, but ultimately, she'd had to face reality. Thankfully, her sister had suggested they move in with her family in exchange for Sara's help in reworking Camille's small business. It had seemed like the perfect solution. As the visual manager of a large department store, Sara had the skills necessary to turn the shop into a showplace.

"I'm going to let you go. Can't wait to hear your ideas."

Sara slipped her phone into her pocket and turned her attention back to the cluttered store. The number of items crowding the floor made it impossible for the eye to find a place to land. No wonder business had never taken off. People liked to see things presented in a way that sparked their imagination or stirred a fond memory. The New Again Emporium had the potential to be a first-class business, but it needed style. And lots of it.

It was so typical of her sister to act without thinking things through. Camille looked at the fun and glamorous parts of an idea and none of the work involved. She'd fancied herself as the owner of a shop on the downtown square, greeting customers and playing the perpetual hostess, obviously never sparing a thought for the long hours, the constant rearranging of merchandise or the paperwork required.

Sara started as a clap of thunder exploded overhead. Storms had been forecast for the entire day. As the sky outside darkened, so did the interior of the old building, casting eerie shadows over the lifeless space. Shaking off the sense of unease and trying to ignore the storm outside, she opened her laptop and made a few notes, then adjusted her timeline. She needed to take measurements of the space and make a cursory inventory of the merchandise to see what she had to work with.

It was late afternoon when she took a break. The storm had passed, and she'd accomplished all she could for now. The enormity of the task ahead weighed heavily on her mind. Sara smoothed her hair behind her ears. It would take several days just to catalog the merchandise Camille had amassed, and she hadn't even explored the second floor yet.

The light outside was almost gone, deepening the shadows in the large store and making her aware of how alone she was. A shiver chased along her spine. Time to go home. The place had a creepy feel in the twilight and conjured up memories of the scary movies she used to enjoy.

Quickly she gathered up her belongings, eager to leave the empty store. She'd managed to do a good bit today but not the most important thing. She'd found no inspiration. Normally at this point her imagination would be vibrating with ideas, but all she felt was overwhelmed.

A scraping noise sent her heart into her throat. She glanced toward the rear entrance of the store. She moved forward and peeked out into the kitchen. The back door opened onto a small parking lot, but it was Sunday. No one should be coming by today. Her heart pounded. She froze in place as tendrils of fear slithered along her spine. The sound came again. The door moved. Frantically, she searched for a weapon. The store had been closed a while and someone probably thought it was an easy target.

Not on her watch.

Her first impulse was to hide and self-protect, but she decided to stand and defend. Grabbing a poker from a fireplace tool set, she held it out like a sword. The door opened wider, and panic squelched all her bravado. She ducked behind a large armoire to regroup. Coward. She had to safeguard herself and her sister's store. She stepped around the wardrobe to see a man carrying a large ornate mirror. He looked huge, with dark hair and a gaunt, angular face. His ice-blue eyes reminded her of a wolf's. The bulging muscles in his arms flexed as he positioned the mirror against the kitchen counter. Determination overrode her fears.

"Stop. Don't come any closer. I've already called the police."

He braced, squaring his shoulders and looking even more threatening. This was a stupid idea. She should have just hidden and let him take what he wanted.

His wolflike eyes narrowed, and a muscle in his jaw flexed. "Who are you?"

The nerve of the man. "I'm the owner of this store."

He shook his head. "No, you're not."

He slipped his hand into his back pocket. Was he reaching for a gun? "Don't move. I'm warning you."

He raised his brows. "Lady, I'm just here to…"

"Steal a valuable antique?" Sara had no idea if the mirror was worth anything or not, but why else would he be taking it?

"What are you talking about? I'm returning it."

She scowled. "Your conscience get the better of you? Well, returning property you stole won't keep you out of jail. You'll be going away for a long time for that."

"Lady, I don't know who you are or what kind of funny juice you're on. Just give me my money and I'll be on my way."

"You want me to pay you for returning something you stole? I think you're the one on funny juice. Get out." She took a step toward him, thrusting the poker. "Now." He shook his head like she was a silly child. Furious, she pulled her phone from her pocket and took a quick snap of the thief. "There. The police will be able to find you easily now. There's no place to hide. They'll track you down like a skunk."

The man's eyes darkened, and his mouth pressed into a tight line. "I'll be back for my money."

"Ha. I don't think so. I'm going to hire a

guard to watch over this store, so don't think you'll steal anything from here ever again."

The man turned on his heels and walked out. She hurried to the door, slamming it shut and locking it. Resting her forehead on the metal surface, she waited for the adrenaline in her system to dissipate. Her heart was still pounding when she turned around. The front door. A jolt of alarm chased along her nerves. What if he came around to the main entrance and tried to come back in?

Her apartment building back in Chicago had been burglarized, and she'd vowed to be vigilant going forward. She hurried to the wide-windowed front of the store, locked the double doors, then scanned the sidewalk outside for the thief. Convinced he was gone, she inhaled a deep breath and dropped into a pale pink side chair.

Thunder rumbled across the sky again. Another round of storms was coming through. Lightning cracked overhead, further unsettling her nerves. She needed to go home.

Now.

Luke McBride pulled his black pickup to a stop in front of the old barn he used as a workshop as his friend and manager, Fred Peters, came toward him. Luke climbed out and gave his friend a shake of his head. "I almost got arrested."

Fred scowled. "I hope you're kidding."

Luke shrugged a shoulder. "Partly. I went by Camille's place to drop off that mirror, and there was some woman there who thought I was trying to rob her. She brandished a poker at me."

"Who was she and why was she in the store?"

"Beats me. She refused to let me explain and then she threatened to call the police." He exhaled. "She took my picture."

Fred scratched his short beard. "Uh-oh. Not good."

"Tell me about it." Luke turned and walked into the shop. The knot that had formed in his chest when the woman took his picture had grown. He leaned against the workbench, gauging his next move. The woman's threat to call the police had chilled his blood. He couldn't afford that. He'd finally started to feel comfortable in this town. The last thing he wanted was for his past to be dredged up and ruin everything he'd built in Blessing. He had to find out who she was and why she was in Camille's store.

"I know that look. What's got you worried?" Fred slid his hands into his pockets.

"That picture she took. What if she sent it to the sheriff's office?"

"Yeah. Your face popping up at a police station, even a small one like here in Blessing, could be awkward. Why don't you call Camille and see what's up? She should know if someone new is working at the store."

Luke nodded. "Yeah. Maybe I will."

Fred gave him an encouraging punch on the shoulder. "Let me know what you find out. How are the benches coming for the Blessing Bridge Park?"

"One more to build. They'll be done by the next workday." The bridge was a local landmark and had been a sanctuary for Luke from the first day he'd come to town. The site was undergoing a restoration, and he'd volunteered to build several benches to place around the newly landscaped grounds.

Fred smiled. "They'll be a welcome addition. I'm glad to see you getting more involved in the community."

"I'm not involved. My benches are."

Fred shook his head. "Luke, boy, you've been here almost three years. Don't you think it's time you crawled out of your hole and joined the world again?"

Luke's protective shield shifted into place. "I'm working on it. One thing at a time."

Fred smiled. "Okay, just remember, you're not alone here. You have me and you have Him." He cast his gaze upward.

Luke nodded. His faith was part of his daily life now, but it wasn't that long ago that he had ignored it. It had taken a death, an arrest and hitting rock bottom for him to find it again. His newfound peace with God was the only thing that had made moving forward possible. He was now content and comfortable and secure. He saw no reason to mess with that formula.

Luke glanced at the old Victorian table in need of a new leg. He'd already turned it on the lathe, but he wasn't sure he could get the stain to match with the rest of the piece. Provided, of course, Camille still wanted it repaired. She'd closed her store a few months ago, so he wasn't sure what her future plans would be.

Had she sold the business? Was that why the strange woman was there? The whole thing would have been funny if she hadn't taken that picture. She'd blindsided him. She'd been like a little terrier, holding him at bay with an old poker and refusing to back down. It wasn't until she'd mentioned the police that his heart had started to race, and his past flashed before his eyes.

When she'd taken his picture he'd almost grabbed the phone from her hand, poker or not.

But then he'd looked into her brown eyes and seen the raw fear. She was terrified. Of him? He didn't want that. There'd been enough people fearful of him in the past. He'd decided it was time to retreat. It wasn't until he was on the way home that he realized the woman might actually report him. He couldn't risk her following through on her threat.

She had warned him he'd be hunted down like a skunk. Despite his worry, he couldn't help but smile. Really? A skunk?

There was nothing he could do right now. For the time being, he'd have to hope nothing would come of her threat. He'd been safe for three years, and he had to trust that the Lord would protect him now. A visit to the Blessing Bridge for some quiet prayer time might be in order. He'd make a run down there before supper. He was overdue.

Sara dropped her purse and laptop case on the bench inside the back door of her sister's renovated farmhouse. Camille smiled at her with anticipation.

"Welcome home. I can't wait to hear all your ideas for my shop."

Sara took a seat on a stool at the island. "What's the crime rate here? I thought small towns were supposed to be safe."

"They are. Why?"

"Because you were nearly robbed." She held up a hand. "I chased him off. He turned tail and ran when I threatened to call the police. You'll need to get new locks just to be on the safe side."

Camille stared at her in surprise. "Are you sure? There hasn't been a robbery here in ages."

"He was trying to make off with a large mirror. I took his picture for the police. They'll track him down. He won't be robbing anyone else."

"A mirror?"

Sara studied her older sister. "Are you okay? You look a little pale. Maybe you should lie down."

"What did the man look like?"

"Big. Mean. Nasty. Wait. I'll show you his picture. I think we should hire a guard. It's not safe there alone."

Camille took the phone, glanced at the photo, then closed her eyes and tilted her head backward. "Oh, Sara. You didn't."

"Didn't what?"

"That's not a thief. That's Luke McBride, my carpenter. He took the mirror a while ago to repair. He was bringing it back."

"You know him? Why didn't you tell me he was coming today?"

"I didn't know. He comes by when the job is done. I gave him a key so he could return things when it was convenient for him."

Sara didn't know whether to be relieved or furious. "He scared me to death. I threatened him with a poker."

Camille sank onto a stool, her hand on her cheek. "I can't afford to upset him. He's the only one skilled enough to repair the old pieces I have in the store." She rested her hand on her pregnant belly. "I'm trying to convince him to build the café, but he hasn't agreed yet. I hope you haven't scared him off."

"What café?" Her sister had never mentioned anything about a café.

"Oh. Didn't I tell you about that? I'm going to put in a small café in the front of the store right by one of the plate glass windows. It's going to be so cute."

As her sister described the café, Sara's creative juices started to flow. "That's a really good idea, sis. Would it be a full restaurant?"

Camille shook her head. "No. We have plenty of those in Blessing. This would be a place where friends can come to grab a light lunch or have coffee and pastries during the day. We'd only be open for lunch on Friday and Saturday at first, with a limited menu. We can always expand later."

Sara smiled. "I like it. And they can shop before and after they eat. Keeping people in the store is the key to increasing your business. This could really be a huge boost to your store."

"You really think so?"

"I do."

Camille sighed. "But it'll only work if Luke agrees to take on the job. He hasn't given me his answer yet. And now…"

"I might have ruined everything." Sara laid her hand on her sister's. "I'll fix this. Don't worry. I'll call and apologize and make it right."

"I just hope he'll understand. I really need him to remodel the kitchen so I can prepare the food and construct the eating area up front. It has to be open for the Bicentennial Arts and Crafts Festival."

"Is that a big deal?"

"Yes. This entire year has been one big event

each month, all building up to the main celebration this spring. I want the store to be a part of that."

"Then I'll call him right now."

"Actually. I think it would be best if you went in person. Luke isn't a talk-on-the-phone kind of guy. He lives right next door. He's our neighbor."

Sara swallowed, her gaze drifting toward the window. Next door? Too close. She wasn't in any hurry to meet the guy again. Not only for the embarrassment involved, but because something about the man made her edgy. Maybe she could find another contractor to do the café work and avoid McBride completely.

She forced a smile. "Then I'll stop by tomorrow before I go to the store, but remember, if I find a job…"

"I know. You're leaving. I'll be grateful for any help you can give."

"And I'm grateful for you giving Jonah and me a place to live in the meantime."

Camille came around the island and gave Sara a hug. "Thank you for coming to my rescue. I knew I'd made a mess of the store. I always do. I don't have the business sense you do."

"Nonsense. You haven't made a mess of

anything. It's all fixable. The most important thing is taking care of yourself and those precious babies. I'll handle all the rest."

"I'm so glad you're here. I've missed you."

"Me, too." Despite the loss of her job and being dependent on her sister, Sara was glad to be together. She'd forgotten how good it felt to have family to rely on. She'd do her best to save the store, and if that meant dealing with the scary McBride man, then so be it.

Her heart felt determined, but her emotions were churning when she pulled to a stop at the end of Luke McBride's driveway the next morning. She chewed her bottom lip. This was the last place she wanted to be. Confronting the man again and trying to explain her behavior yesterday wasn't going to be easy. She'd tried calling other contractors to see if they could take on the café build, but with no luck. She had no other option but to try and make amends. All that really mattered was that she leave here with a promise from McBride to build the café.

Pressing on the accelerator, she steered her car between the row of trees lining the drive, which widened out in front of a large barn with a scattering of outbuildings beyond. Off to one side, atop a small rise, stood an old brick Victorian farmhouse with a rickety front porch.

She scanned the area but there were no signs indicating where she should go. As she exited the car, a gentleman approached from around the side of the red barn. Wiry and slender, he had a short gray beard and smiling eyes.

"Good morning. Can I help you?"

"I'm looking for Mr. McBride."

"He's in the shop. Follow me. I'm Fred Peters, the sidekick around here."

Sara liked the man immediately. "I'm Sara Holden, Camille's sister."

He stopped at the door. "Pleased to meet you. Camille and Dave are good friends of mine."

Fred opened the door. The loud drone of a motor made it hard to hear. He flipped the light switch off and on quickly. The noise ceased, and Sara spotted the carpenter across the room, near a large workbench. He turned and met her gaze, causing a small lump in her throat. He removed his safety glasses but didn't move.

Fred started forward and Sara followed. "Luke, boy, this is Miss Sara Holden. Camille's sister. She needs a word with you."

Fred nodded, then walked off, leaving her alone with the scary man. Only he didn't look scary at all today. He wasn't huge like she'd thought, but maybe a tick over six feet. The muscles she'd labeled as bulging were more the product of a well-defined physique. He came toward her, and she had to adjust another misconception. His eyes weren't wolflike at all. They were a shade of blue that reminded her of a summer sky. In fact, as she looked at him now, he was more handsome than horrifying.

"Camille's sister, huh? Come to make a citizen's arrest?"

Heat flooded her neck. "No. I'm here to apologize. I had no idea who you were."

He wiped his hands on a rag. "You would have if you'd allowed me to explain."

"Yes, I know. But I was scared."

"Which is why you picked up the poker."

Sara winced. "Bad move, I know, but I was alone, and I thought…" He was fully aware of what she'd thought. "My apartment complex was broken into a month ago, and I guess I overreacted." She opened her purse and pulled out an envelope. "Camille sent this." She held it out. "It's payment for the mirror."

He hesitated a long moment before stepping closer and taking the envelope from her hand. "Thank her for me."

"Mr. McBride, I am truly sorry for my behavior yesterday. I thought I was protecting my sister's store."

"From a dangerous criminal."

Sara swallowed. Clearly, he was not going to make this easy. "Yes, at the time."

McBride shoved the envelope into the side pocket of his tan carpenter pants. "Are you always so aggressive?"

"No. Well, it depends. The point is, I'm so sorry. I hope you won't let my foolishness keep you from working with my sister. She thinks highly of your skills and considers you invaluable to her business."

"Why would I blame her for your mistake?"

"Hopefully, you wouldn't. I also want to ask you to please consider building the café in the store. It's very important to Camille, and I think it will be a big boost to her business, especially if it can be completed for the festival."

He shook his head. "I don't know. I'm not sure I can find the time. What's your interest in the café?"

"That's why I'm here. I promised to redesign the store and increase business."

"You're the new manager?"

"No. I'm just making the place more visually pleasing. I'm a visual merchandising manager at a large department store. Well, I was until the store was bought out by a competitor, and my job was eliminated."

Luke studied her a long moment. "Do you plan on threatening customers you don't know?"

Her cheeks flamed. "No. Of course not. Please tell me you'll accept my apology. I promised Camille."

"So, you don't really feel sorry. You're just trying to make your sister happy."

She frowned. Was that a smirk on his face? And was that a twinkle in his blue eyes? "Mr. McBride, I am truly sorry for the misunderstanding. I thought I was being robbed. I acted on instinct."

"Did you call the police after I left?"

"No. Of course not, though I intended to until Camille told me who you were."

He turned and walked back to his workbench.

Sara waited. She needed to know she'd succeeded. "Mr. McBride, will you…"

"Apology accepted." He replied without looking at her.

She took a step forward. "And the café?"

"I'll think about it."

"I hope you'll decide soon. Time is running out, and my sister has her heart set on the café being ready for the festival."

He turned and held her gaze. "I'll think about it."

She'd been dismissed. Her impulse was to keep trying to convince him, but she had a feeling any attempt to push this man too hard would only make him dig in his heels. She turned and headed toward the door, her gaze falling on a table that stood off to one side. She took a closer look. The wood grain on the top was stunning, and the gracefully turned legs were amazing. Even in its unfinished state, it was an exquisite piece of woodworking. "Did you make this?" She trailed her fingers across the smooth surface.

"Yes."

"It's beautiful. Who's it for?"

"No one."

She turned to look at him. "Then why did you build it?"

"For my own satisfaction."

Sara frowned at his response. "People would pay top dollar for this craftsmanship."

"Not interested."

Sara allowed her gaze to drift around the large workshop, coming to land on the loft above where more tables and other pieces of furniture were stored. "And those? Are those for sale?"

"No."

Was the man nuts? "I don't understand. Why build things you don't intend to sell?"

"I have my reasons." He turned his attention back to his work. Conversation over.

Sara started toward the door, her mind filled with questions. What kind of man built beautiful things, then hid them in a hayloft? Not the kind she wanted to get to know. Her hand was on the doorknob when Luke called her name.

"I'd appreciate it if you'd delete the photo you took."

It was an odd request. "Why?" The look on his face said he wasn't about to give an explanation. But it was clear it was more of an order than a request. "Yes, of course."

He slipped on his safety goggles and went back to work, and she headed for her car with no idea if she'd made things better or worse for her sister. She also had a lot of questions about Luke McBride. No matter how hard she tried, she couldn't for the life of her understand building for personal enjoyment when the furniture could be enjoyed by others. It was the height of selfishness in her book, and she'd had her fill of selfish men.

Chapter Two

Luke tried three times to figure the materials list for his next project before he gave up. The last person he'd expected to see in his shop today was the odd lady with the poker. And he surely hadn't expected her to be his neighbor. His gaze drifted toward the door. She looked different today. Shorter. Prettier. Granted, his first impression was distorted by the poker in her hand and the threats she'd been making, but now that the terror was missing from her eyes, he could see they were a warm brown color and filled with passion.

He tossed his pencil on the workbench. Time for a break. As he passed the table he'd finished yesterday he thought about Miss Holden's comments. He'd seen a glint in her eyes that suggested she hadn't been satisfied with his response.

Fred entered the barn through the side door, a knowing smile on his face. "So, the mystery lady turned out to be Camille's sister. Interesting. So why was she here?"

"To apologize. And to ask me to remodel the kitchen in the store for that café Camille wants."

"Will you?"

"I don't know. It's not my usual type of job."

Fred nodded. "True. Building alone in this old barn is more your style." Fred adjusted his cap. "Luke, boy, I think you should take the job. It would do you good to branch out, and you'd be doing a favor for people who have been your friends since you moved here."

Luke couldn't deny that. "It would mean working with the sister. That alone is a reason to say no."

"Afraid she'll call the police when you make a mistake?"

"No. But I did ask her to delete the photo. I just wonder if she will."

"No reason for her to keep it." He patted Luke on the back. "Stop worrying. I'm heading to the hardware store. Anything you need?"

Luke shook his head, his thoughts still drifting to that picture. Fred was probably right—she'd have no interest in hanging on to the photo. He'd grown paranoid over the last few years, but it was time to let go of that.

Luke's gaze drifted to the table again. He couldn't get over how different the sisters were. Camille Atkins was tall, slender and full of energy, with light brown hair and hazel eyes. Sara was shorter, curvier, with deep brown hair that swayed against her chin and intelligent cinnamon-colored eyes. She was the loveliest woman he'd ever met.

The unexpected attraction alarmed him. He didn't need anyone in his life. He had everything he needed on this farm. His woodworking gave him a purpose, he had a good friend to share his time with and a quiet, unobtrusive existence in a town that barely registered on a map.

He didn't want anything to disrupt his peace. And he had a feeling a woman like Sara could easily upend his carefully arranged life, which was the main reason he didn't want to build the café. It would put him and his work out there for others to see and expose him to questions and attention he didn't want. He'd had enough publicity and humiliation to last him forever. The scandal had not only cost him his sense of self but the stress had been the cause of his beloved grandfather's demise.

The light in the barn flickered later that afternoon, and Luke shut off the sander and glanced over his shoulder at his friend, frowning at the expression on the older man's craggy face. "What's up?" Fred stroked his short beard, a gesture Luke knew meant he was troubled about something.

"I've been trying to get hold of your finance guy, but he's not returning my calls. I've left messages for the last several days. Any idea what's going on? He's not usually this hard to connect with."

Luke nodded. "As a matter of fact, I think he mentioned he was taking a trip, but he should have been back by now." A brief spark of concern rose. Mike Horvath had handled his finances for years. It was because of him that Luke had been able to emerge from the scandal with a secure future. He'd made it possible for Luke to buy the farm and not have to worry about getting a job. Unless something changed, like a woman who sent his photo to the police.

"I'll try and track him down. I'm sure he's just busy."

Luke turned his attention to the table he'd just finished and ran his palm over the surface. Smooth as glass. Next step was to decide which stain color to apply. He wondered what

Camille's sister would like. A dark rich color or a lighter, more natural tone?

He groaned and turned around. What had put that thought into his head? Something about Sara Holden had taken a spot in his thoughts, and he couldn't get her out. It had nothing to do with how attractive she was; he was only concerned with that picture she'd taken. Had she deleted it?

Fred turned to leave, then stopped. "Oh, Luke, boy, Taylor Lumber called, and your pecky cypress has arrived. You want it delivered or will you pick it up?"

"I'll get it tomorrow."

Fred took a step closer. "What's eating at you? Oh, wait. Let me guess. Camille's lovely sister."

Luke shook his head. Fred had been his friend from the moment he'd first toured the farm. Over the last three years he'd been an advisor, a sounding board and a voice of reason Luke had come to rely on. But sometimes that closeness gave Fred insight Luke didn't really appreciate. "I hadn't noticed."

"Then I'd better take your pulse." He came to Luke's side. "Have you thought any more about building that café Camille wants?"

"No."

"I think you should do it. It would showcase your work for the town to see better than the few repair jobs you've done. It'd be a good challenge for you. It's only for a few weeks, and you can win Sara over to your side."

"Why would I want to do that?"

Fred shrugged and grinned. "Maybe because you're still in knots wondering if she really deleted your picture."

"What if she hasn't? What if she…"

"Luke, you're making a mountain out of a mole hill. I told you, no one down here cares a whit about something that happened in Chicago."

Fred had a point. Luke had lived the last few years of his life looking over his shoulder, avoiding people, only venturing out into the world a small step at a time. The fear, no, the horror, of facing again the kind of exposure and humiliation he'd endured during the trial was crippling.

If he were honest, the idea to branch out had started to come up more and more. Maybe Fred had a point. The café job would showcase his work but also keep him sequestered with only Sara to deal with. He couldn't avoid a normal life forever. Perhaps this was the next small step in becoming integrated into the community. And it would give him the opportunity to make sure Sara deleted his picture.

Sara unlocked the back door to New Again and laid her purse and satchel on the small table in the break room just as her cell rang. "Hey, Camille."

"Did you talk to him? Is everything okay?"

Sara considered her words. "He accepted my apology. I think he understood what happened."

"And the café?"

"I stressed how important it was to you and how it could mean the difference for the success of the store." She paused a moment. "He said he would think about it."

"Sara, I need an answer. If we don't start soon I won't make the opening in time."

Sara fiddled with the clasp on her satchel. "Maybe you should plead your case. He's not very receptive of me."

"Big surprise there. Honestly, sis, thinking that man was a robber…"

The comment brought a couple of questions to mind. "He asked me to delete the picture I took of him. Don't you find that a bit strange?"

"No. It probably wasn't a very flattering photo."

"I guess. Do you know why he doesn't sell his furniture?"

"What are you talking about?"

"His shop is filled with beautiful furniture, but when I asked him who they were for, he said he builds for his own satisfaction. Why wouldn't he sell what he's made?"

"I don't know. What does it matter?"

Sara sighed. "It doesn't. I was surprised, that's all. His work is amazing. It just seems odd that he hides his light under a bushel, so to speak."

"All I want to know is if he'll take on the café."

"I'll try again in a day or so. Don't worry." Sara ended the call and closed her eyes. She'd given her sister a positive review of her meeting with Luke, but inwardly she had serious doubts. Luke McBride didn't strike her as a jump-in-and-help-a-friend kind of guy. Quite the opposite. Something about his attitude raised red flags. He seemed too concerned about that photo she'd taken. Why on earth would someone with so much skill crafting fine pieces of furniture not sell them? Who did that?

She had no answers, but she did have decisions to make. Scanning the room, she focused her attention on the sales floor. Her goal today was to tag all the best pieces to use as focal points and draw up a layout. She had no idea how she was going to move some of the larger pieces, but she'd find a way, even if she had to hire help.

After supper that evening, Sara went in search of her son. Jonah had been so preoccupied with his cousin that they'd had little time together. She found him on the back porch tossing a ball to Daisy, the family's yellow Lab. She took a seat on the steps beside him. "Hey, sweetie. How's it going?"

"Good."

Her gaze drifted out across the broad sloping lawn and the pond with its wooden dock and the grove of trees at one end. "Looks a lot different here than Chicago, doesn't it?"

"Yeah. It's neat."

The enthusiasm in his voice was disconcerting. "How did school go today?"

He turned, a big smile on his face. "Great. I like going to school with Rusty, and everyone is really nice."

She didn't like the sound of that. She'd vowed to give her son the best education possible. One structured toward an Ivy League college. A public school in a small Missississippi town was not in her plan. There was no way Jonah could maintain his current level of achievement here. By the time she got him back into private school he'd be a year behind. Maybe she could find a tutor to help him in the meantime.

Was it possible that her son actually liked living in the country? She kept her tone light to mask her deep concern. "You know, your old school was one of the best in the city. I'm sorry we had to leave it behind."

"I'm not." Jonah shrugged. "I hated wearing a uniform."

Stunned, she stole a quick look at her son. She had no idea he'd felt that way. What had she missed? She could tell by Jonah's posture he'd withdrawn. Quickly she searched for a neutral topic. "I can't believe you learned to ride a bike so quickly. That's amazing."

Jonah shrugged and petted the dog. "It was easy. Rusty only showed me how once. I learn quick when I want to."

"I'm proud of you. But be careful. Wear a helmet. Don't go too fast and…"

"Mom. I'm nine. Not a baby anymore, okay?"

It was true. Her son was growing up. In

the short time they'd been at her sister's, he'd learned how to ride a bike, fish and climb a tree, and made friends with Daisy. Jonah had never shown an interest in any of those things before. He'd been content to do his school work and attend the various activities she'd scheduled for him. Every time she turned around, her son was attempting something new and keeping her in a constant state of worry.

She had to find a job soon before Jonah grew more attached to Blessing. She might be forced to change her plans where the store was concerned, but she wasn't about to change her plans for her son's future.

Rusty bolted out onto the deck. "Have you asked her yet?"

Sara glanced at her son. "Asked me what?"

"I want to play on Rusty's football team."

Sara opened her mouth to refuse but Jonah pleaded his case.

"It's flag football, no tackling. Please, Mom. Practice starts this Tuesday."

Camille joined them. "Honestly, sis, it's perfectly safe. Lots of running but no rough stuff."

Sara glanced between her son and her nephew, and the anticipation on their faces was her undoing.

"I guess it'll be okay." The boys whooped

and ran into the yard, tossing a football back and forth. Camille patted her shoulder.

"Face it, sis, our boys are growing up, and we can't keep them under our thumb forever."

Sara watched the boys play. They were happy. But she had to think beyond today. She stood and went inside, trying to ignore the truth of her sister's words. She couldn't control Jonah's every move. He was getting a mind of his own, and she wasn't prepared.

Her fears about living in a small town grew. The more things Jonah got involved in, the harder it would be to leave when she found a new job. The rejection she'd received this afternoon, however, had her worried. She was running out of retail businesses to contact.

She just had to cast a wider net, that was all. And be patient.

Sara stood at the front of the store the next morning and let her gaze travel over the eclectic assortment of furniture. Her ideas were slowly coming into focus. The main obstacle was getting the larger pieces into the right areas. The only bump in the road was the café seating area. If it was built, then she had less floor space to work with, which wasn't a bad thing. But if it didn't, then she had to make sure that space in front of the window was filled with enticing displays to draw the customers inside.

Her phone rang, and Camille's name appeared on the screen. Her heart skipped a beat. She tried to hide her worry from her sister, but her concern for her pregnancy was always at the forefront of her mind. "Hey, sis. Everything okay?"

"Everything is perfect. I just got a call from Luke. He's agreed to take on the project. He'll be there in a few minutes to get started. Finally, everything is coming together."

Sara forced a happy tone in her voice. "That's great news."

"I know. He's stopping by to pick up the blueprints, then he'll head to the store. Don't threaten him with a poker when he shows up."

Sara chuckled, but it had a hollow sound she hoped her sister wouldn't notice. "I'll be nice. I promise." Of course, that depended on how you defined *nice*. She glanced at her schedule for the day. Having the carpenter in the store all day could seriously impede her work. Sara set her hands on her hips. Nothing irritated her more or threw her off her game than surprises and sudden changes in her plans. Her gaze went to the back of the store and the wall separating the sales floor from the kitchen and other workrooms in the back. All she had to do was keep to her space and ignore him. No problem.

Turning her attention to her work, she wound her way through the furniture toward the back corner, where the pieces had been shoved up against the wall and covered with a stained canvas drape. She sidled between a bookcase and a stately secretary and tugged off the canvas. A small gasp escaped her. She reached out and touched the table that had been hidden beneath.

"Oh my. Aren't you a beauty?" The round table was one of the most stunning she'd ever seen. The top was an intricate inlaid design with mixed woods all radiating from the center. She bent down to inspect the pedestal. It too was a work of art. Her spirits lifted. This could be her focal piece for the front of the store. Her creative juices fired up. She tugged on the table, but it wouldn't budge. There was no way she could move it without first getting all the other pieces out of the way. Even then she might not be able to drag it to the front. At Crowley's Department Store, she'd always had in-store help to wrestle the big pieces. Here she was all alone.

"Hello. It's Luke McBride. I'm coming in."

Sara puffed out a breath. Great. She finally had a spark of enthusiasm and now she had to deal with him. "I'm out front."

"Unarmed?"

She made a face. Was he trying to be cute? She made her way toward the back. She'd say a quick hello, then leave him to his work.

"I have a surprise for you."

Sara stopped in her tracks, her irritation spiking. "I don't like surprises." She stepped into the back room. "Let's get one thing straight right off. I hate surprises." She crossed her arms over her chest. Luke was standing at the kitchen counter with a puzzled expression. She tried to ignore the sudden skip in her pulse. He looked good in carpenter pants and a plaid shirt that matched the blue of his eyes. She choked off that thought.

"Not ever?" He lifted one eyebrow.

"Never. Surprises mean change. They mess up plans. They complicate lives. Nothing good comes from them. I don't like being blindsided." His eyes narrowed. "If we're going to work together you need to remember that."

Luke nodded slowly. "Okay. I guess that means you aren't interested in these fresh cinnamon rolls I picked up from Blair's Bakery?"

He opened the lid of a foam container, and the room filled with the sweet scent of cinnamon.

The tantalizing aroma made her realize she hadn't had breakfast. Then her embarrassment kicked in, and her cheeks warmed. He'd come with a peace offering, and she'd attacked him. Again. "I'm sorry. I wasn't expecting… I mean, I didn't think…"

"That a thief would bring a gift?"

Sara pressed her lips together, wishing she could disappear into the floor. "No. It's…" She had no explanation other than a bad first impression and some questions about his behavior.

"Miss Holden—"

She shook her head and moved toward him. "Call me Sara. Maybe we should start over. You're going to be here every day for a while. We need to feel at ease."

"I agree. So, Sara, can I offer you a cinnamon roll?"

Sara smiled and nodded. "Thank you. That was very kind of you." She took two plates from the cupboard and forks from the drawer. Luke leaned against the counter to eat his, and she decided to do likewise. Sitting at the small table seemed too cozy. "Thank you, for agreeing to build the café. My sister is so excited."

"Camille and Dave have been good friends. I was happy to do it."

Sara wanted to ask why, if they were such good friends, it had taken him so long to decide, but she didn't want to muddy the waters. "Okay. Where do you start?"

"Here in the kitchen. Most of it will be demolished. Afraid it'll be noisy in here for a few days. Hope that's okay."

Sara forced a smile. "Of course." What else could she say? Hopefully, the wall between his work space and hers would be enough of a buffer.

"So, I have to ask, why the intense dislike of surprises? Most people enjoy them."

Sara stared at her half-eaten roll. She should have known her reaction would raise questions. "It's not the surprise as much as the secrets behind them. It starts when someone is hiding something, then it's exposed and lives are destroyed, left in ruins."

She braved a look at Luke, anticipating the same puzzled look she received whenever she tried to explain how her marriage ended. Her gaze locked with his and her heart stopped. There was understanding in his blue eyes, as if he actually understood the damage secrets could cause. Her nerves quivered as if there was a physical connection between them. She didn't realize she was holding her breath until he broke eye contact and turned away.

"I get it."

How did he know? Had there been secrets in his life? She wanted to ask him, to find out what had happened, but her common sense came into play. She wasn't ready to share her past with him, so there was no reason he should share his with her.

Luke opened his toolbox. "I'd better let you get back to work."

"Right. Me, too. Thank you for the treat."

"You're welcome."

He smiled, and her pulse kicked. How had she ever thought he was a big, scary man? Funny what fear did to an otherwise rational brain. As she made her way to the front of the store, she kept wondering why it had taken Luke so long to make up his mind about the café. Did it have anything to do with his reluctance to sell his furniture?

She shook off the notion. None of her business. All that mattered was he was on the job and he'd made her sister happy. Now it was up to her to make the store shine. She'd barely cleared a spot near the front door for the table she'd found when pounding and sawing began.

It sounded like Luke was knocking down a wall. Was he? It didn't matter. The café really had nothing to do with her part of the store.

Her gaze traveled to the space in front of the plate glass windows where Camille said the seating area of the café would be located. Before she could begin organizing the merchandise, she needed to know the exact perimeter of the café.

A loud bang shook the air, followed by the sound of splintering wood. Surely the man could work more quietly than that? She marched into the kitchen and stopped in her tracks. All the upper cabinets were gone, the stove had been pulled out into the center of the room and the sink was sitting on the floor. "What are you doing?"

Luke straightened and frowned. "Demoing the kitchen."

"How is Camille supposed to prepare food without a sink or stove?"

"She can't. She can't use these appliances, anyway. They aren't up to code. She has to meet health codes to open a food service business."

The sound of a heavy truck penetrated the brick wall. A loud clanging sound followed.

"What was that?"

"The dumpster being delivered."

"Dumpster?"

He shrugged. "You have to toss all this debris someplace."

Sara saw her plans being shifted again. If Luke was making this much noise tearing the kitchen apart, what would the rebuild sound like? A wave of discouragement settled on her shoulders. At Crowley's things had always been civilized and elegant, with soft music playing in the background. She'd been calmed by the atmosphere. Camille's store was anything but calming. It was a jumbled mess with no direction. Now it was loud and filled with dust.

Unable to find words, she waved her hand in the air and went back to the front, stopping at the area she'd earmarked for the lovely round table. There was no way she could move it by herself. She needed a pair of strong shoulders. Shoulders that were right now working in the kitchen.

She groaned and rolled her eyes. Asking for his help was like admitting she wasn't capable of doing her job. But the truth was, she couldn't. She had to remember that getting the store open again was her first priority. Even if that meant stifling her pride and asking for help from the carpenter. No matter how much it went against the grain.

Slowly she made her way back to the kitchen. Luke was nowhere to be found, but the back door was wide open. And the debris on the floor had dwindled.

"You looking for me?" He stepped inside, meeting her gaze.

She hesitated. "Uh, yes. I was wondering if you could show me exactly where the café seating is going to be. I need to know how much space I'll have left to work with on that side of the store."

"Sure." He retrieved a tape measure from his toolbox, then picked up the blueprints and started toward the front.

She followed. He spread the plans on an old buffet table and leaned over to take a closer look. "Okay, according to this, the café will start about here, three feet from the door casing." He pulled off a piece of blue tape and attached it to the wall. "It'll extend out to about here, then over to the wall. The opening is right in the middle of this area." He placed a small *X* on the floor with the blue tape. "Does that help?"

She now had an idea of the space that would be taken up, but at the moment that area was filled with odds and ends she hadn't figured out what to do with yet. "Yes, but is there some way we can make the marks more visible? I need to see the space easily as I'm rearranging the merchandise."

He glanced around and then picked up a coa-track and placed it on one of the pieces of tape, then he retrieved a floor lamp and placed that on the far mark. With a flourish he attached the tape between them, creating a makeshift rope to cordon off the proposed café space. "Better?"

"Very. Thank you."

"Anytime. Anything else I can do for you?"

He was being very accommodating. Not at all like the grim, withdrawn man she had to apologize to. "Well, as a matter of fact, there's a table I need to move, and it's very heavy. Maybe you could give me a hand?"

"Lead the way."

Sara wound her way through the large furniture and squeezed behind the secretary. "This one." Luke's eyes widened, and he reached out to stroke the tabletop. "Nice."

"I know." She smiled, pleased that he recognized the workmanship. Coming from a skilled woodworker, it affirmed her opinion. "It's going to be the first thing customers see when they enter the store."

"That should impress them." He glanced over his shoulder, then back at her. "I'm guessing you want this at the front door, then."

"Yes."

Without a word he shoved the other furniture aside to make a path for the table. "Want to give me a hand?" He lifted his side, and she did her best to hold up her end, but the table was not only heavy but cumbersome. She had to set it down twice before they got it to the front.

The moment it was set in place Sara knew she had her focal point. "Perfect." Her imagination took flight. Tomorrow she'd start going through the smaller items upstairs and see what kind of decorative pieces she could find to highlight the piece.

"Thank you. I think I can finally start pulling this place together."

"With one table?"

"No. That's the inspiration piece. Once I have it decorated I'll get another idea, then another, and before long it'll all come together."

"If you say so." He looked skeptical.

"You don't understand retail merchandizing."

He frowned. "It's old furniture. You put the

tables and chairs together, the bookcases in one spot and the armoires in another."

"I would have thought you'd have more imagination, being a creative person."

"I'm not creative."

"You build beautiful furniture. What do you call that?"

He shrugged, the movement emphasizing the breadth of his shoulders and sending heat into her cheeks.

"Following a plan. I cut out the pieces and put them together."

"You're underestimating yourself. Don't you think your work is good enough? Is that why you don't sell them?"

Luke's mood shifted. "I don't need to."

"Wow. Must be nice to be independently wealthy."

Luke set his jaw. "I have to get back to work. Let me know if you need anything else moved."

"Thanks. I will." Sara watched him walk back to the kitchen, her curiosity growing. How could he not consider himself creative, and what had she said that had killed his helpful mood? It was like he threw up a shield of some kind. Did it have something to do with his reasons for not selling his furniture? It was definitely a sore point with him. But why? What did he have to hide?

Dismissing that train of thought, she resumed her search through the furniture in the area Luke had marked off. It had to be cleared eventually. The banging and sawing resumed, and she covered her ears. Maybe she'd get used to the noise.

Maybe not.

Chapter Three

Luke turned his attention to hauling the demolished kitchen to the dumpster out back. He'd hoped the physical exertion would keep Sara off his mind. She was the curious type, and that wasn't something he wanted to deal with. She didn't like simple answers to questions. She wanted details, backstory, reasons. If she kept this up, working with her the next few weeks could prove problematic.

An unexpected twinge of regret tugged at his thoughts. Despite himself, Camille's sister intrigued him, and it was more than her girl-next-door allure. She was determined and focused on her goal. He admired that in anyone. She was dedicated to making her sister's store a success, and she was doing it all alone.

Luke had tried to lighten the tension that had

lingered between them. He felt responsible for that. When she'd stopped by his shop to apologize, he hadn't been very receptive. He'd been too concerned about that picture she'd taken. Fred had made him realize that he was probably overacting. His trial and conviction were three years ago. It might have been a media circus in Chicago, but in the south Mississippi town of Blessing, it had probably never made the local news.

Luke had decided it was time to stop looking over his shoulder every minute for reporters hiding in the bushes. His life has been quiet and uneventful for the last several years. Moving to his grandfather's hometown had been a wise choice. Taking on Camille's project was a smart decision, too.

He'd told Sara he built his furniture for his own satisfaction, and he hadn't lied. The process of constructing each piece allowed him to heal from the emotional trauma of the past and find a new direction for his life. He'd recently considered branching out and taking on more jobs from paying customers, even toying with selling all the pieces he'd crafted. But he didn't want to risk becoming too successful. That would draw attention, could open up a Pandora's box of trouble.

The café was an experiment. He'd take on the job and see what came of it. Working with Sara was concerning, but he'd brought pastry that first day in hopes of showing her he was willing to let bygones be bygones. How was he to know that the woman hated surprises? Really hated them. Her tone had been icy, and her brown eyes shot sparks in his direction.

The disturbing thing was that when he looked into her eyes, he understood precisely what she was experiencing. He ached for her. No one should have to go through that kind of trauma. What was her story? What painful surprises had rocked her world? What secret had reared its head and brought her world crashing down around her ears?

He smiled as he went back to work. He found her emotions delightful. A man would always know where he stood with a woman like her, unlike the hot and cold, confusing personality of his ex-wife. He'd never known what mood she'd be in when he got home or if she'd even be there. He shut down that line of thought. It always led to a dark place that was hard to come back from.

"Luke."

He spun around as Sara came toward him. "I found some chairs in the back of the store, but I need help moving the things in front of them."

"Lead the way." He followed her past a collection of chairs to the far corner, where two of them had been shoved behind a large roll-top desk and an old mantel. He maneuvered them out into the open. "What was wrong with those chairs?"

She frowned and gave him an are-you-serious expression. "Wrong style."

"Isn't a chair a chair?"

"No." She picked up one chair and started toward the front. He followed with the other.

She set hers beside the round table he'd moved earlier. She smiled and stepped back. "See. These are perfect for this table. The other chairs were too rustic."

Luke set his hands on his hips. "I don't see the difference."

"Thankfully, I do."

He scowled. "Right. You decorate stores."

Sara raised her chin. "I do. I did. Unfortunately, a lot of department stores are cutting their visual staff. It's making it hard to find another job. When Crowley's was sold to a competitor they didn't need two visual managers, so I drew the short straw."

Luke's pulse leaped. He knew that store. It

had been his wife's favorite place to shop. "You worked for Crowley's?"

Sara smiled and nodded. "Their flagship store in Chicago."

Luke's mouth went dry. "How long were you there?"

"Seven years."

Luke's protective shield shot into place, and he moved away from Sara. "I need to get back to work."

She looked at him in surprise. "Okay."

He could see the questions exploding in her mind. He had to get out of here before she started asking them. He strode to the kitchen and tried to catch his breath. Sara would have been living in Chicago during his trial and all the media frenzy that had followed. Quickly, he gathered up his tools and fastened the metal toolbox. He had to leave. He needed time to think and sort out what he'd do next.

"Luke? Are you leaving so soon?"

He nodded without looking at her. "I have another job I need to take care of. I'll be back tomorrow." Would he? Working with Sara had taken a new turn. Maybe he should go and tell Camille he couldn't do this job. It was too risky.

"Oh, all right. I'll see you then. Thanks for the help."

He cringed at the curiosity in her voice. And that prompted him to ask a question of his own. One he needed the answer to. "Did you...delete that picture you took?"

"Yes. I said I did. Why?"

Bad move. He should have left well enough alone. "Just checking." He picked up the toolbox and made a beeline for the door. "See you later."

He walked briskly toward his truck, climbed in and closed the door. What was he going to do now? What if Sara recognized him? What if she got curious and started probing?

Luke ran a hand down the back of his neck. He'd learned two important things about Sara Holden. She was curious and she hated secrets. That was a dangerous combination because he was a man with secrets.

Luke's sudden departure and his request again to delete his photo had circled around in Sara's mind the rest of the day and was still nagging at her as she drove Jonah and Rusty to flag football practice that evening. She'd even retrieved Luke's photo and studied it but could see no reason for him to be so upset. She doubted he was a man who was vain about his appearance, so there had to be another reason.

A thousand questions flooded her mind but only one really mattered. Why he'd left so abruptly was less important than would he return to finish the café? What would she do if he backed out?

Sara set those worries aside as she parked the car at the ball field. Jonah and Rusty bolted from the car and raced toward the other children gathered at the edge of the playing field. Sara followed behind. As she approached the small stand of bleachers, a familiar figure caught her attention. Luke. What was he doing here? This was why she didn't like surprises. It was always best to be prepared, and surprises didn't allow that.

Jonah ran to her. "Mom, Mr. Luke is going to be our coach. Isn't that cool?"

Stunned, Sara stared at her son. "How do you know Luke McBride?"

"He's Rusty's neighbor. We ride our bikes on his dirt piles, and he fishes with us at the pond."

He turned and dashed back to the other players, leaving Sara's thoughts in turmoil. How did she not know what her son was doing? Sara let her gaze drift toward the dark-haired man surrounded by energetic kids. How did he keep turning up in her life, and what was she supposed to do now? Did she go and speak to him or behave as if his presence was of no importance?

The matter was taken from her hands when Luke looked in her direction, nodded, then turned his attention on his players.

"Are you Rusty's aunt?"

Sara looked at the woman who had come to her side. "Yes. I am."

The woman smiled. "And Jonah's mother. I'm Marilyn Parks. My daughter, Ellie, is on the team and a classmate with the boys. Come sit with me. We can watch practice together." She smiled. "The time goes faster if you have someone to talk to."

The last thing Sara wanted at the moment was to chitchat with a stranger, but at least it would keep her mind off the flood of questions about Luke that kept spinning in her mind.

Marilyn leaned toward her. "It was nice of Luke to fill in as coach for the rest of the season."

"He's not the regular coach?"

"No. Our coach was called away for work, so Pastor Miller asked him to step in for the last few games. The season is almost over.

Let's just hope he can keep us winning. We're looking at a championship in the league."

Sara pondered that information. It was at odds with her impressions of Luke. Yet as she watched, she saw a different side to the man as he interacted with the players. Very curious.

Marilyn offered her a bottle of water. "You're Camille's sister, aren't you? The one working at New Again?"

"I am."

"We are all so excited to have the store open again. My mom used to work for the previous owner. She really hated to see the place sold. Do you think it'll be open soon?"

"That's my plan. My sister really wants it up and running for the Arts and Crafts Festival."

"That would be wonderful. I loved wandering through that store. So many lovely things. I always came away inspired to redecorate."

That was exactly the thing Sara wanted to hear. The chitchat ended as the kids took the field, and Sara focused her attention on Jonah, her heart in her throat and praying every moment for his safety. To her surprise, the football game consisted mainly of running up and down the field. She discovered that Jonah was fast. He'd made it to the goal with the red flag still on his belt. Rusty snatched the flag off the opposing team to save a touchdown. The cousins whooped and hollered and chest-bumped each other.

There had to be something in the male DNA that made them want to clobber each other in happy moments. Even Luke got into the spirit of things by sharing high fives with the kids. The smile on his face was one of pride and joy. Strange how the smile gave her a funny sensation in the chest.

Marilyn leaned toward her. "You know, I drive right by your sister's place on my way to practice. I can pick up the boys if you need me to."

Perfect. "Yes. Thank you. That way I can stay longer at the store."

And she could avoid Luke and that unsettling smile of his.

Sara glanced at the clock the next morning before turning her attention to the buffet table she'd shoved up against the wall. Was Luke coming to work today? Or had he decided to abandon the project? She had no idea what to expect. She hadn't told her sister about Luke's abrupt departure the other day. It would only worry her.

Marilyn Parks had proved entertaining and

helpful. She'd explained the finer points of flag football to her and extolled the coaching prowess of Luke McBride. Sara had been intrigued by the different side he'd displayed on the field. He clearly enjoyed coaching the kids, and they responded to his direction eagerly. Jonah had sung his praises all the way home.

None of that eased her concern. If Luke didn't return, she had no idea how she'd get the café completed. She wasn't going to let her sister down.

She stepped back and studied the small arrangement she'd made. She needed to find a few more pieces, but when it was completed, it would be charming. Her next project was to set up a sitting area with the Victorian settee she'd found, but only if Luke showed up to help her move a few things around.

The back door opened, and she jerked her head toward it, willing Luke to enter. She blew out a breath of relief when he stepped into the kitchen. Thank goodness. She made her way toward him, sorting through the right words to say. "Good morning."

He faced her, his gaze holding hers and sending an odd sensation skittering along her nerves.

"Morning."

She rubbed her palms together. "I wasn't sure you'd show up today."

He kept his back to her as he unfastened his toolbox. "Why's that?"

"Well, you left rather abruptly."

He glanced at her briefly. "I explained I had another job."

"I know, but…"

Luke set his jaw. "If you're worried that I might back out of this project, don't be. I always finish what I start. No matter the circumstances."

Something in his tone intrigued her. "Good to know."

"If there's nothing else, I need to get to work."

"Of course. Me, too."

The rest of the day passed with little interaction between her and Luke, which only added to her anxiety. She walked on eggshells all day, worried that she might say something that would upset Luke and he'd walk out for good. He left at the end of the day without even saying goodbye, which tightened the knot of worry in her chest another twist and made for a stressful evening with her sister while she tried to act as if nothing was wrong.

After supper, she retreated to the family room and took a seat in the wooden rocker near the fireplace, enjoying the quiet. The boys were up-stairs watching a movie, Dave was in his office and her sister was puttering in the kitchen.

A deep sigh escaped her lips as she leaned back in the chair and closed her eyes. The rock-ing eased the tension of the day from her body. Her fingers gently rubbed the silky-smooth surface of the arm. It reminded her of the table she'd seen in Luke's workshop.

Camille strolled into the room. "You look comfy."

"I am. This is the most comfortable chair I've ever sat in."

"I'm not surprised. Luke built it."

Sara took a closer look at the rocker. She should have guessed it was his work. "I thought he didn't sell his furniture."

"It was a gift for some legal work Dave did for him." Camille patted her shoulder. "I'm turning in. I'll see you in the morning."

Sara nodded, her mind whirling with a new idea and a plan that could make her sister's business a destination shop far into the future.

But it all depended on Luke and her own powers of persuasion.

Luke made sure he was at the store early Thursday morning, hoping to be deep in his work when Sara arrived and avoid any small talk. Unfortunately, he'd received word that the plumbers would be on-site today. He'd have to explain the situation to her. She wouldn't like it, but then, she probably had no idea about how the construction process worked. Maybe there was something he could do to help her in the store today.

He heard the front door to the shop open. Sara had arrived. She always preferred to enter through the front door, for some reason. She looked up and smiled as he approached. His heart skipped. Seeing her each morning was like waking up to sunshine. Today she had on a light pink top over her faded jeans, and the color matched the blush in her cheeks. The shine in her brown eyes spoke to her enthusiasm, and her smile always brightened the space around her. "Good morning, Sara."

"Hello. How are you?"

"Good. I need to let you know that the plumbers are on their way. They should be finished around lunch if all goes well." Her smile faded and her eyes narrowed. He'd surprised her again. Not a good start to the day.

"What does that mean exactly?"

"We'll be without water for most of the morning."

"I can still work, can't I?"

"Sure. I'll be taking up the floors in the office and storeroom. If you need any help just let me know."

"Before you go, I'd like to talk to you."

Luke raised his brows. "About what?" Had she found him out? Was she going to fire him? His abrupt departure yesterday had probably triggered her curiosity. He set his jaw and braced for the worst.

She hesitated a moment. "I sat in one of your rockers last night. It was the most comfortable chair I've ever been in."

"Thank you. It was a gift to Dave and Camille."

"She told me. I've been looking for a signature piece of merchandise to feature in the shop. Something that would draw people from miles around. One unique item they could only find here in Blessing at New Again."

He had a bad feeling he knew where this conversation was headed. He opened his mouth to respond, but she continued.

"How did you manage to design such a perfect chair? The seat is the perfect depth, and the back is at the perfect angle. It's amazing."

Luke slipped his hands into his pockets. "I didn't design it. My grandpa did. He was a master carpenter. He worked for years getting that rocker perfected."

"And he taught you?" She smiled at him, her eyes warm and soft.

"In a way. He taught me woodworking, but it took me three tries to get the rocker right, even following his plans."

"It must have given you a great sense of pride and satisfaction when you finished."

"I suppose."

"Something that perfect should be available to everyone."

Her motives were becoming clear. He shook his head. "I'm not selling you one of my rockers."

"I'm not asking you to sell me one. I want to sell them for you."

Luke studied her a moment. What was she talking about?

"I want to feature your rockers in the store on consignment. It would be a mutually beneficial arrangement. It would help the store, and you could make a nice profit."

He shook his head. "Out of the question. My rockers aren't for sale."

"Maybe I didn't make myself clear. I'll do all the work. The marketing, the promoting, dealing with the customers. All you have to do is provide the rockers."

He should have known she wouldn't take no for an answer. "Not happening." He started to walk away, but she grabbed his arm. Her small hand landed on his bare skin, and the tingle her touch created was unsettling. For some reason he was reluctant to pull away.

Sara swallowed and went on. "But your chairs are a perfect fit for this store. We're made for each other."

Her words conjured up an image he wasn't prepared to consider. He stepped back. "No. We aren't."

"Luke, one of your chairs could save this store. We'd be the exclusive dealer for the Mc-Bride Rocker. It would change the way people think about the store and put you and your woodworking on the map."

"What makes you think I want to be on any map? I have no intention of selling my rockers, and even if I did, it wouldn't be through a store on the town square. You'll have to find some other piece of furniture to peddle to the locals." He pivoted on his heel and strode to the kitchen. The sight of the half-done space and the amount of work still needing to be done was overwhelming. Now more than ever, he regretted taking on this job.

Grabbing up the long-handled pry bar, he

shoved it under the edge of the wood floor and began prying it loose from the subfloor with more force than necessary. He needed to keep busy and away from Sara. He knew she would continue to push, and there was no way he could explain his reasoning without getting into areas he wasn't about to discuss. The trouble was, he didn't think Sara would let the subject drop. His refusal would only fuel her determination. The same determination he'd admired when it came to her work in the store was now the trait that might unravel his world.

Strange thing was, part of him really wanted to help her make the store a success, but not at the expense of his past coming to light.

Chapter Four

❧

Sara watched Luke march away, her throat clogged with regret. What had she been thinking? She'd handled that all wrong. She had a bad habit of assuming everyone would catch her vision and come along the way they had at Crowley's. But there, she'd been the boss. They'd had little choice but get on board. Luke wasn't one of her employees. She should have broached the subject, then waited for the idea to settle in before pushing forward.

Running her hand through her hair, she kicked herself mentally, then regrouped. She'd let some time pass before bringing it up again. Maybe, after they were more acquainted, she could make him understand how successful the store could be. And him, too.

Sara kept busy for the rest of the morning,

shoving Luke and his reaction to the back of her mind. She couldn't keep worrying he'd walk off the job. He'd vowed to complete the work, and she had to take him at his word. He was making a racket in the back removing the floors. But the noise was reassuring, since it meant he was on the job.

It was midafternoon when she realized the noise had ceased. She headed to the back and met the plumbers on their way out. They gave her a quick rundown of the work they'd performed and left.

The office was free of flooring, but Luke was nowhere to be found. His toolbox was gone, which told her he'd gone for the day.

Back on the sales floor, she sat at the make-shift desk she'd put together with a small table and bookcase, her gaze focused on her planner, her frustration mounting. She'd accomplished only a small portion of the things on her list. Luke was always causing disruptions. But she needed him. What should she do now? Did she owe Luke an apology, or should she simply take a step back and give time a chance to sort things out?

Her phone chimed and she scooped it up, tensing when she saw Camille's name on the screen. Had Luke pulled out of the project and was Camille calling to demand an explanation? Sara braced for the worst. "Hey, sis."

"Hello. I was just checking in to see how things are going."

Sara sighed inwardly. At least she had genuine progress to share. "Going great. The plumbers were here today, and the electricians are coming tomorrow. Things are rolling along."

"Oh, I wish I could come and see. Are the cabinets in yet?"

Sara tried to remember the things Luke had told her. He was very good at keeping her informed about the various stages of construction and what to expect. She just hadn't paid much attention. "Luke and Fred are building the cabinets at the shop, but they can't install them until the plumbing and electric are done and the inspectors approve everything."

"Do you think everything will be done in time for the festival?"

"Of course. Luke has it all under control."

Sara prayed she wasn't giving her sister false hope. Following an impulse, Sara sent Luke a text, asking him if he'd be back to the store today, claiming she needed help moving a few things. An hour later he still hadn't replied, and her concern grew.

Determined to salvage the day, she set her mind to arranging a few vignettes, then spent the afternoon on the second floor sorting through the boxes of decorations and the wide selection of mirrors and wall art. By the end of the day she'd found enough items to highlight the furniture downstairs, and her creative juices were flowing full force.

For the first time since setting foot in The New Again, Sara had a plan coalescing in her mind and excitement fueling her energy. Tomorrow she'd start fine-tuning the groupings of furniture she'd arranged. She had the next two days planned out, and she couldn't wait to get started. This would put her back on her original schedule and back in control. For the time being, she'd set her worries over Luke aside and enjoy her job.

Her cell rang as she climbed into her car. Camille again. "I'm on my way home, sis."

"Good. I meant to ask you, could you please go to the Blessing Bridge Park Saturday morning and help out? It's a big volunteer day. I was supposed to go, but of course I can't in my condition."

Sara sighed, her plans melting away again. "Camille, I have so much to do here I shouldn't leave."

"I know, but it's important, and it'll show how committed I am to supporting the town."

As much as she hated to admit it, her sister had a point. Being visible at community events was a good marketing tool. "Fine, but don't be upset if this puts me behind."

"I'm not worried. You were always at your best when you were overcommitted."

Sara didn't bother to point out that she was usually in that position because her sister always dumped her chores onto Sara. Camille usually had something more important or fun to do.

Some things never changed.

Luke and Fred set the wooden bench in place near the full-grown southern magnolia tree and stood back to wait for Katie Unger to approve the location. Katie was in charge of the restoration of the Blessing Bridge Park, and she had a clear vision of where everything should go, right down to the flowers.

"Perfect. Thank you, Luke. Your benches are going to get a lot of use. We'll secure them in place so they can't be moved." She smiled. "The design is perfect for the park. We deeply appreciate your donation."

Luke nodded. "My pleasure. I'm glad to give

back to the park. It's been a blessing to me many times."

"Amen." Fred nodded in agreement.

Today was a big volunteer day at the Blessing Bridge Park. The long-neglected land and the old bridge were getting a complete restoration for Blessing's upcoming bicentennial. This was the final push. Flowers were being planted, structures painted and fresh sod laid in bare spots.

"We have one more to get off the truck. Where do you want it?"

Katie pointed toward the gazebo on the hill a short distance away. "There's a stake with a red tag."

Luke and Fred hoisted the next bench from the truck and made their way to the designated spot. They had just positioned it when Luke glanced up and saw Sara standing a few yards away. The look of confusion on her face sent his pulse jumping. They hadn't spoken since she'd approached him about selling his rockers. He'd ignored her texts all day yesterday, and he was feeling guilty about that. He should have responded, but he wasn't ready to explain or face the curiosity in her eyes. Friday, he'd spent working on the cabinets, soothing his conscience with the knowledge he was still on the job, just not on the job site. Besides, the electricians were there, and he didn't want to get in the way.

Fred leaned close. "Did you know she was going to be here today?"

"No." There was no escaping her now. Time to face the music.

Luke held his breath as Sara slowly approached. His nerves were wobbly, the way they'd been when his mother had caught him doing something he shouldn't. The soft fawn color of Sara's eyes was nearly black when she met his gaze.

"What are you doing here?"

He cleared his throat. "I delivered a few benches for the park."

She glanced at the wooden bench. "You made these?"

He shrugged. "I wanted to make a small contribution."

Sara pursed her lips together. "I see. You won't sell your furniture, but you'll give it away or donate it?"

"That's right." Luke quickly turned the tables. "What are you doing here? Taking a break from the store?"

Sara raised her chin. "Not on purpose. I should be there now, not here planting flowers.

There's so much to do. As you know. Actually, I'm filling in for Camille. She had signed up to help today but obviously she can't now." She crossed her arms over her chest. "You didn't answer my texts."

"I've been busy, building benches and cabinets for the store." Luke pressed his lips together. Sara was wondering if he was still working for her. "I'll start installing cabinets this week. Don't worry. Everything is on schedule."

"Good. I can't fall behind. I don't want to let my sister down."

"Understood." She started to turn away, then stopped and glanced over her shoulder. "Have you thought anymore about my suggestion? Your rockers in Camille's store would be a win for both of you."

Luke squared his shoulders. "Still not interested."

She pressed her lips together, and he could see she was preparing to argue. She must have thought better of the idea because she gave him a small insincere smile instead. "I'd better go. I'm supposed to be planting flowers around the tree."

She walked off, and Luke exhaled a pent-up breath. He knew Sara didn't understand his reasoning about his woodworking. How could she? But explaining his position wasn't an option. Selling his work could lead him down a path he never wanted to travel again. No matter how much he wanted Sara to understand. For reasons he wasn't sure of, he didn't like being in conflict with Sara, but that was becoming a frequent event, and he had no idea how to change it.

Later, as Fred drove the truck back to the farm, Luke stared out the passenger-side window, his thoughts traveling in circles. "Sara wants to sell my rockers in the store." He hadn't intended to share that with Fred, but he was getting dizzy trying to sort things out.

"Oh? What did you tell her?"

"I turned her down, of course." Luke stared at his friend. "You know what kind of trouble that could create."

"Do I? What was her offer?"

Luke explained Sara's plan.

"How did she take the rejection?"

"Not well."

Fred grinned and nodded. "It sounds like a great idea. She's taking on all the work, and all you have to do is haul the rockers to the store. You have nearly a dozen of them. And it would be another step forward to getting you out of your cave."

"I don't live in a cave."

"A barn, then." Fred shook his head. "Sooner or later you have to step out of the past and hold your head up and face the world. Stop acting like you're guilty. You're not."

Maybe not, but he felt like he was, every day when he woke up. The memory of the stares, the cameras, the jury, the walk into the prison, were always close to the surface of his mind. They even overshadowed the day he walked out a free man. "I agreed to take over the flag football team, didn't I?"

Fred chuckled. "One giant step for man."

Back in the barn, Luke couldn't shake his friend's observation. He did feel the pull to shed the past and move forward. And Sara's offer had held a measure of appeal. It would be a good solution. He could be free to build and let her deal with the public. But first he had to get over the big question. What if? What if he started drawing attention and someone discovered that the man who made their perfect rocker was a convicted murderer?

Luke strode to the fridge and pulled out a beverage. Would he have to start dodging reporters again? Would the networks be pulling up his driveway with their cameras and satellite trucks? He didn't want to see the suspicion in people's eyes, feel them pulling away in fear, turning their backs and locking their doors.

No. Stepping out of his comfort zone wasn't an option. Not now. Not ever.

Sunday morning dawned with warm sunshine, a gentle breeze and colorful pansies on display in every yard. Camille held Sara's arm as they walked up the steps at the front of the Blessing Community Church. Jonah and Rusty had already headed for their Sunday school room, and Dave had arrived early to see to his deacon duties. It was the first time her sister had been out in over a week, and she was bubbling with happiness.

Sara waited while Camille stopped and talked to people who greeted her with smiles and hugs. Camille made friends so easily. It was one of the qualities Sara envied. It had always been more difficult for Sara. Even today, most of the people she was close with were more work colleagues than real friends.

"Good morning."

Sara turned at the sound of Luke's deep voice. She hadn't expected to see him here. "Hello."

"You look surprised to see me."

"No. I mean… I guess…" She swallowed. "I didn't think you went out in public much."

"I make an exception for church. And the ball team."

A half smile lifted one corner of his mouth, unleashing a small flock of butterflies in Sara's stomach. She looked around for her sister, who had drifted off down the sanctuary aisle and was taking a seat in a pew. "I'd better join Camille." She turned away, then glanced over her shoulder, a question on the tip of her tongue.

Luke held her gaze. "Yes. I'll be at the store in the morning."

A rush of heat filled her cheeks and warred with her relief and irritation. She didn't like that he could read her mind and how his presence stirred unwanted emotions. It took all her willpower to keep from turning around during the service to see if he was still in the sanctuary. Thankfully, the pastor presented a sermon that captured her attention with his topic of shame and forgiving one's self. Once God forgave the matter, it was closed. Nothing could be gained by continuing to feel ashamed of past events and decisions. Hanging on to the guilt meant you were not trusting in the Lord's grace.

* * *

The next morning, Sara found herself still thinking about the topic of the sermon. Trusting was something she found difficult to do. Too many people had let her down too many times. She shook off the bad memories and turned her focus to her work. Taking hold of the vintage étagère, she dragged it across the floor and positioned it beside the green velvet settee. Once she added the old floor lamp and the petite tea table, she could start gathering knickknacks to display. That was her favorite part: adding the pretty stuff to her small groupings. She'd discovered a treasure trove of glassware, figurines and china upstairs. She planned to concentrate on the furniture groupings she'd arranged over the last few days. There were still sections to work out, but she was ahead of schedule. Provided, of course, Luke finished his work on time. He hadn't started on the café seating area yet, which bothered her.

Her gaze drifted to the back of the store. It was silent this morning. No plumbers or electricians. No Luke. What would she do if he didn't show up?

The creak of the old back door broke the silence, and her heartbeat jumped. She held her breath until she saw Luke walk toward her. "Good morning." Her voice sounded breathless.

He nodded. "Morning."

She forced a smile. "What's on your agenda today?"

Luke set his toolbox on the board laid between two sawhorses. "Framing up the new walls and laying flooring in the office and break room."

Sara bit her lip. "How long will that take?"

"We'll be done tomorrow or the next day."

She thought about how much there was left to do. The kitchen was a mess, and time was moving quickly. "We can't afford to fall behind."

"We won't. Fred finished the cabinets yesterday, and the appliances will be delivered when we let them know. It's all under control. If you need any help moving things around, just say the word."

The friendly tone in his voice filled her with relief. Their relationship was back on track. Thankfully, her suggestion hadn't chased him off. "Thanks. I'll take you up on that. I still have some large pieces to shift around."

"Give me a shout."

Luke went back to the kitchen, and Sara allowed herself to relax. Having him back on the job lifted her spirits and spurred her enthusiasm. She decided to tackle the next display she'd envisioned. Using the massive Art Deco bookcase as a divider, she could create a small reading nook that would showcase the old library table, the easy chair and the footed sewing basket. With a few choice table decorations and some vintage textiles, the vignette would be adorable.

Sara slid the pallet dolly under the bookcase and slowly lowered the lever, raising the bookcase off the floor. She pulled it toward the space she cleared in the far corner.

The bookcase wobbled when she hit a rough spot in the floor. She held her breath. She'd have to move more slowly or the bookcase would fall. Taking a deep breath, she tugged on the handle. It didn't budge. She yanked harder.

"Sara!"

Too late she saw the bookcase wobble. She gasped and extended her arms knowing it was a futile gesture. She wasn't strong enough to hold the piece upright. An arm appeared in front of her face, and the bookcase stopped moving. Sara found herself staring into Luke's blue eyes.

"Are you all right?"

The concern on his face acted like a switch releasing her emotions. Tears sprung into her eyes, her body shook and she nodded. "I think so. I didn't… I wasn't…"

Luke gripped her shoulders. "It's all right. You're safe."

She closed her eyes, feeling a sense of security in his touch. She hadn't felt like this in a very long time, and she was in no hurry to relinquish it. Until she remembered it was Luke offering her comfort. She took a deep breath. "Thank you. You saved my life."

Luke smiled that crooked smile of his. "Well, from a nasty fall at any rate. Why didn't you get me to help you?"

"I thought I could do it myself. I've moved several big pieces with that dolly."

Luke rested a palm on the side of the bookcase. "This is top heavy. It needed extra support."

She nodded. "Next time I'll have you help. Promise." She realized she was still holding Luke's forearms. She'd stepped out of his embrace, but he didn't let go. Her gaze locked with his, and she was acutely aware of his masculinity. The breadth of his shoulders and the strength in his hands sent a trickle of appreciation along her pulse. The warm light in his blue eyes tempered that observation with a more impactful one. He cared what happened to her. The realization was puzzling. Did he find her attractive? She hoped so. The thought was startling.

"Yo! Luke boy. You here?"

Fred's gravelly voice broke the spell. She turned away, taking a few deep breaths.

"In here. I could use your help."

Within a few moments, Luke and Fred had positioned the bookcase in its spot.

Luke smiled. "Anything else you need?"

She cleared her throat, not wanting to follow that line of thought. "As a matter of fact, there is. I'd like your opinion on something."

Luke set his hands on his hips. "I always have an opinion on things."

Sara ignored the odd skip in her pulse as she led him to the back wall of the sales floor. "I found this old hutch, and I'd like to salvage it somehow. It could be adorable if it were restored."

Luke frowned. "Adorable?" He opened the lower door, and it came off in his hand. The small drawer was stuck shut. "Why would you want to save this? It's junk."

Sara pressed her lips together. "I know it needs work, but it has a nice shape, and I think it could be very attractive with a little love."

Luke shook his head. "It would be easier to start from scratch."

"I thought you were good at fixing old furniture."

"I am. Some things can be saved or reworked, but sometimes it's best to start over."

Fred walked up and smiled at her. "Hello."

"Hi, Fred." She gave Luke a sideways glare. "Fred, what do you think of this old hutch? I see potential. What do you see?"

Fred made a quick examination. "Well, it's in bad shape, but I don't think it's ready for the junk heap yet. What were you thinking?"

She rested her hand on the side. "Maybe new lower doors. I found two old grates that might look good, and then replace this old shelf and use bead board for the sides."

Luke shifted position and sighed. "I tried to tell her it would look like junk. There's no way to put new wood and old wood together and make it look decent."

Sara gritted her teeth and focused her attention on Fred, who had an expression she recognized: imagination at work. He winked at Sara, forcing her to stifle the smile teasing her lips and the sharp words perched on the tip of her tongue.

"No, now, wait a moment. I think she may

be onto something." Fred used his hands to illustrate his idea. "We could make new doors and rout a channel for the grillwork. As for this counter, I'm sure we could find an old piece of marble or granite that might do the trick."

Sara's excitement swelled. Finally, someone who saw her vision. "Yes. And we can leave the upper part old and weathered, very farmhouse style. I love it." She turned in unison with Fred to face Luke. Sara fought not to laugh. He looked puzzled and a bit confused. Clearly, the whole concept was lost on him.

Fred chuckled. "Why don't you let me take this to the shop and work on it? If it's all right with Luke."

Luke held up his hands in a gesture of surrender. "It's your time to waste." He turned and walked away.

Fred patted her arm. "Luke's a little slow on the uptake."

"I noticed."

"We'll load this up later. I'd better get to work."

Sara gave the older man a quick hug. "Thank you. I just know this will be something unique."

Fred gave her a thumbs-up. She followed slowly behind him, her gaze searching out Luke. He was back in the kitchen, fully focused on his work. For someone so talented with construction, the man had zero imagination.

Hopefully, he would make up for that with his work ethic.

Luke drove the screw into the sheet rock, then set his drill on the floor. He could report to Sara that all the drywall was installed and ready for taping and floating. Though she'd still be uneasy about how long this remodeling process took. No one was ever prepared for the work to take twice as long as expected, and it always did.

Maybe he could appease her by starting on the café seating area. That section should come together quickly. It only consisted of a decorative railing installed around the perimeter to separate it from the sales floor. Camille had asked him to turn the spindles himself. So far he'd only completed a portion of them. He needed to get back at it if he didn't want to fall behind and incur Sara's wrath. She liked things done on her schedule even if it was unrealistic. He smiled. Despite himself, he admired her fierce determination.

He had no doubt that once the tables and chairs were in place and decorated with Sara's imaginative ideas, it would be a big draw for the store.

Luke glanced over at Fred, who was adding the last pieces of drywall to the new office. They made a good team, and Luke appreciated that the man went about his work quietly though he wasn't a taciturn man by nature. Fred could talk up a storm when he was inclined—he'd been chatty enough with Sara earlier.

What had his friend seen in the old hutch that he'd missed? Watching the two of them as they talked about the dilapidated cabinet and the excitement that had bloomed between them, he'd felt excluded. He was content with his relationship with Sara. She did her job and he did his, with little interaction. But each day, he'd found it harder to corral his attention when she was nearby. She had a soft way about her when she worked, a deliberate but gentle approach to her designs. When she completed a display the smile on her face was sweet and adorable.

Witnessing the instantaneous connection between Fred and Sara over the old hutch had unleashed a small pang of envy in his chest. He wasn't sure why that bothered him. His gaze drifted to the far corner of the building where Sara was putting books on the shelves in different configurations. Even from here, he could sense the energy in her movements. She really loved tinkering with all this old stuff. His mind replayed the moment he'd seen the heavy furniture start to tilt. He didn't remember moving, but somehow he was holding the piece upright, before it could fall on her. Fear still sparked through his veins when he thought of what might have happened.

Holding her close, feeling her heart race, had forced him to acknowledge that his attraction to her was growing. He needed to control his emotions. This might be a good time to work on those spindles. He'd have Fred fill in at the store for the next few days, and he'd work from the shop. It would give him time to get his head on straight.

"Ready for spackling." Fred patted his shoulder and nodded toward the walls. "This place is going to be really nice. Can't wait to see it filled with customers."

Luke nodded. "Me, too." Strangely enough, he meant it.

Fred picked up his toolbox. "I'm going to head back to the shop. You want to give me a hand loading that hutch?"

Luke watched his friend drive away, then

went inside to collect his tools and say good-bye to Sara. He heard her on the phone as he neared her workstation. He could tell by the tone of her voice and the dejected droop to her shoulders that something was wrong. He hoped it wasn't bad news about her sister. He took a step toward her, then stopped, remembering how he resented people intruding into his life when he was upset. Quietly, he started to turn away but she looked up and saw him. "Everything all right? You sounded upset."

Sara brushed her hair from her face. "It's nothing. Just a small glitch in my plan." She smiled. "I need to get to work. There's still a lot to do before we open, and I want the store to be perfect."

He studied her a moment. Her striving to be perfect concerned him. "I'm sure it'll be fine. Maybe you should consider hiring someone to help."

"I am. I need someone to take over when I leave."

Luke's heart skipped a beat. "You're leaving?"

"As soon as I find a job. So far all I have is a long list of rejections."

He'd never considered that Sara would leave Blessing. He knew she was job hunting, but for some reason, he never connected that with her leaving town. "How does Jonah feel about that?"

"What do you mean?"

"He tells me he really likes it here, and he is enjoying the ball team. He's very good for never having been on an organized team before."

"It wasn't possible with my job."

Luke held her gaze a long moment before finally looking away. Silence draped around them like a shroud. Luke cleared his throat. Maybe she didn't understand how her son felt. "Did Jonah talk to you about the clubhouse?"

"What clubhouse?"

"The boys want to make a clubhouse in the old storage shed next to my silo. They plan to fix it up themselves."

Sara's shoulders tensed. "You mean building something?"

"Yes."

"I'm not sure that's a good idea, though. Jonah is too young to handle tools."

"I was ten when my granddad showed me how to build a birdhouse." Luke made a dismissive gesture. "Fred would be doing most of the work, and he'd let the boys help. He taught his sons the trade." He glanced over at her, his tone challenging. "It's what every boy dreams of, building their own secret hideout."

She met his gaze, and her dark eyes narrowed. "Like your workshop?"

Luke knew when to retreat. He'd said too much already. "I'd better go. I have spindles to turn."

He also needed time to digest the news that Sara planned to leave. He'd never considered the possibility. The idea left a chilly spot in the middle of his chest. He steered the truck onto Church Street, his thoughts still tethered to Sara. When had she become such a part of his life? How had he let her slip past his guard and inch her way into his heart?

When had she ignited a spark inside him and given him back something he'd been missing and hadn't realized? Hope.

Sara gave him hope.

He wasn't sure he liked that. Hope was something he'd been short on many times in his life. But what if Sara was a new kind of hope? Hope he could count on?

Chapter Five

It was late Wednesday night when Luke turned off the lathe, removed his safety glasses then leaned in for a closer look at the newly turned spindle. This was the last one. Tomorrow he'd have to go back to the store and start work on the café railing.

A twinge of anxiety skittered along his nerves. He'd shoved all thought of Sara to the back of his mind for the last few days so he could concentrate on work. At least he'd tried to. The memory of the bookcase tilting toward Sara kept repeating in his mind. His heart had lodged in his throat at the idea of her getting hurt. Holding her, looking into her brown eyes, had shifted something deep inside him. Like a rusted lock being opened.

He tried to stop his mind from running on

those lines. There was no room in his life for a relationship. Least of all with a woman like Sara. A woman who wanted openness and honesty. Neither of which he could offer. He ran a hand along his neck. He needed to get this café job done as quickly as possible before exposure to Sara had him longing for things he could never have again.

Luke shut down the shop and headed for the house. He was tired and achy from bending over the lathe and fending off images of Sara. He stepped into the front hall of his home and stopped, suddenly aware of how cold and empty it was. His boots thudded hard on the oak floors as he walked into the parlor. His furniture consisted of a rickety green recliner he'd picked up at the resale store, a small table for holding his drink and a forty-inch big-screen TV perched on top of a wooden crate. Not much of a home.

The 150-year-old Victorian farmhouse had been Fred's family home for most of that time. When Luke had moved in, it was in need of extensive restoration. Fred had kept the house protected from the elements, but it hadn't been updated since the seventies, and it showed.

The silence in the empty room settled upon his shoulders, highlighting the loneliness of the vacant space. When he'd purchased the farm from Fred, he'd intended to divide his time between building furniture and remodeling the house, but somehow he'd kept putting it off, content to keep building his rockers. Fred had accused him of hiding. Not true. He'd needed time to heal and to recover. That was all.

There was a message in there someplace, but he had no desire to dig it out. He turned and went to the kitchen, trying to ignore the sudden edginess he couldn't explain. The harvest-gold-and-burnt-orange decor looked more garish than usual. The only additions he'd made were a microwave, a coffee maker and a few pots and pans. With the exception of the one night a week he and Fred went to the Branding Iron Steak House, he ate his meals in front of the flat screen.

Lonely. The word kept repeating in his mind. "I am not lonely." Hearing the words aloud only made him more conscious of his feelings. What would Sara think of his home? He had no doubt she could turn this sad kitchen into something warm and welcoming the same way she was changing Camille's store. It didn't take long to see that she added warmth and joy to her displays.

Sara had changed the atmosphere of the old

building by simply rearranging furniture and decorating. From cold and unwelcoming to warm and inviting. He could easily see her turning this old house into a home and making it a place to feel safe and content. The way he used to feel in his workshop. Lately, that emotion had become more elusive. Now he wasn't as content or as satisfied, and he had no idea why. Fred would say he was going through the healing process. Luke would counter that it was a matter of too little sleep.

That, at least, was something he could control. Flipping off the kitchen light he headed upstairs. He didn't need to eat. He needed to sleep.

Unless thoughts of Sara kept him awake.

Again.

Sara placed a big check mark on her to-do list and inhaled a satisfied breath. Work had moved forward rapidly in the last few days. Walls painted, cabinets installed, appliances in place and light fixtures working.

Sara glanced over at the front corner of the café area where Luke was working. He was hammering something high on the wall, his raised arms stretching the knit shirt tight along his back, outlining the perfect V of his torso.

He lowered his arm, holstered the hammer, then glanced over his shoulder.

Quickly, she averted her gaze to hide the flush in her cheeks. She hadn't seen him for a few days. Dave had taken the boys to ball practice. Fred had told her Luke was working on the spindles. He'd come in early today and gone straight to work, and she'd had nothing in need of moving, so they hadn't spoken. She wasn't sure if he was simply concentrating on his work or if he was irked about Fred taking on the hutch project. His reaction had been puzzling. Just when she thought she'd found a comfort level with the man, he'd do something unexpected that left her off balance again.

She stole another glance, and their eyes locked. Her mouth went dry, a sudden rush of warmth infusing her cheeks. It took all her willpower to break her gaze from his. The truth was, Luke was a very attractive man, and she liked looking at him.

She needed to stop this obsession with thinking about Luke and watching him. There was no room in her plan for a man, or a relationship of any kind, for that matter. She turned her attention to positioning the china tea set on the old tea cart and folding the vintage napkins she'd found into triangles. She stepped back to check the arrangement when someone called her name from the back of the store.

"Yoo-hoo, Sara, where are you?"

Sara walked around the old armoire, surprised to find her sister hurrying toward her. "Camille. What are you doing here?"

Camille smiled and handed her the large plastic container she carried. "I've brought you lunch."

"You didn't need to do that. You're supposed to be resting."

Camille waved off her concern. "I'm fine. Dave is outside waiting to take me home, and I'll go right back to bed."

Sara placed the basket on the table in the small office, thankful that this space was usable again. "What did you bring?" She pried off the lid and peeked inside. Camille was an excellent cook. A skill Sara hadn't inherited from their grandmother.

"Maple chicken salad. I've been working on the menu for the café, and I need some feedback, so I brought lunch for everyone. Go get Luke and Fred."

"Fred just left to pick up some materials. It's just me and Luke."

"No problem." Camille pulled out two foil-wrapped plates and placed them on the table along with napkins and utensils. "Go get him. I really need a man's opinion on this."

Sara opened her mouth to protest but knew her sister wouldn't take no for an answer. Eating lunch with Luke, the two of them alone in the shop, was not something she wanted to experience. Her goal was to keep as much distance between them as possible, not get closer.

Camille frowned. "Go on. Dave is waiting."

Sara found Luke still working in the front of the store. His crooked smile appeared when he saw her. "What needs moved now?"

It had become an inside joke ever since the incident with the bookcase. She gave him a smug look. "Nothing. I'm inviting you to lunch."

Luke's smile faded and he held her gaze. She couldn't read his expression, but if she had to guess, he was as reluctant to eat with her as she was with him.

"Why?"

Oh, yeah. He wasn't thrilled with the prospect of an intimate meal, either. "Camille is putting the café menu together, and she brought a sample for us to try." For a moment, she thought he was going to decline, and the sense of disappointment surprised her.

"Sure. I'll be there as soon as I wash up."

Sara's heartbeat increased, but she couldn't decide if anticipation or dread was the cause. The table was all laid out when Sara returned to the office. Luke joined them a few moments later. He took a seat, but the table was small and their knees touched.

Camille clasped her hands together. "Okay, I know most of my customers will be women, but I want to offer something a bit more substantial for the men who might come with their wives. Now, I've given Sara the ladies' version, chicken salad on greens, rolls and a fruit cup. I've given Luke the same chicken salad, only it's on a whole wheat bun with pickle and mayo." She smiled and patted Sara's shoulder. "Enjoy."

Sara looked up at her sister. "Aren't you going to wait for our verdict?"

"Nope. You can give me your reviews later. Oh, and there's a sugar cookie for each of you for dessert."

Luke wasted no time sampling his sandwich, nodding in satisfaction at the first bite. "Good."

Sara smiled. "My sister is a great cook."

Luke grinned and caught her gaze. "Does it run in the family?"

"No. But I excel at ordering takeout." He chuckled and took another bite of his sandwich.

They ate in silence for a long while until Sara grew uncomfortable. She knew from experience that Luke didn't care for small talk, but she couldn't eat with this awkward silence hanging between them. "Any word on when the inspectors will show up?"

"They're scheduled for tomorrow. Things should start moving pretty fast after that."

Sara speared a fresh strawberry. "You think we'll make our deadline?"

Luke nodded. "You should be open a week before the arts and crafts festival."

"Camille will be very happy." And she would be greatly relieved.

Luke nodded. "Fred will hate that he missed this free lunch."

"Camille brought an extra for you to take to him."

The silence between them grew awkward again. Sara debated whether to keep silent or try and start a conversation. She was never good with silence. Luke was obviously enjoying his lunch. Sara frowned. There had to be some way to get a conversation out of the man. She took a bite of chicken salad and forged ahead. "Did you always want to be a carpenter?" She looked over at Luke, surprised to see the pain reflected in his dark eyes.

"No. Never."

Not what she'd expected. "What did you do before?" The moment she asked the question she realized she'd hit a wrong note. Shame heated her cheeks, and she lowered her gaze to her plate. When would she learn that he didn't like personal questions? Unfortunately, she had always been the curious type.

Luke rested his forearms on the table, his fingers rubbing together in a gesture of discomfort. "Structural engineering." He shrugged and picked up his sandwich. "I liked figuring out things."

Sara chuckled softly. "That explains the lack of creativity. The old left-brain thing."

Luke raised an eyebrow but didn't appear to be offended at her jest.

"Are you from Mississippi?"

Luke shook his head. "Kansas."

"How does an engineer from the Midwest end up in a small Southern town building rocking chairs?" She watched Luke curl into himself at her question, and her conscience reared its head.

Luke stared at his plate a long moment. "My grandfather was born and raised in Blessing. I moved here after my wife…died."

Sara inhaled sharply, wishing she'd kept silent. She had been looking for some friendly chitchat. Instead, her inquisitive nature had forced Luke to dredge up pain from the past. "Oh, Luke, I had no idea."

The deep sadness in his blue eyes hurt her heart. He must have loved his wife very much. But she sensed he wasn't telling her everything. She started to pat his hand in a comforting gesture, then decided against it. His protective shield was in full force. If she touched him she might receive an electrical shock. She needed a different approach.

"I understand that. After my husband left, I moved to Chicago. It helped to get away from the memories." Dark pain flashed in his eyes. She held her breath. He was obviously still grieving.

"Sometimes the memories follow you."

Sara poked at her meal, wishing she'd never mentioned the topic.

"What about you? I take it Jonah's dad isn't in the picture at all?"

She almost refused to answer, but he'd opened up to her. The least she could do was share a little of her past. "No. Not for a long time."

"You've done a good job. Jonah is a great kid."

"Thank you. I worry that I'm letting him down." Luke smiled, and Sara breathed a sigh of relief. Their easy connection was in place again, giving her the courage to make a request. "I'd like to get started on the merchandise upstairs. I need to see what I have to work with, but I need someone to help me move all those boxes around. I was wondering if you could work late this Friday and give me a hand."

Luke suddenly squared his shoulders. "Sorry. I'm busy." He pushed away from the table, picked up his paper plate and tossed it in the trash.

Sara blinked. Lunch was over. Once again he'd slipped behind his mysterious shield. She tried to ease the tension in the air. "Oh. Boys' night out, huh?" She smiled, but he kept his back turned.

"Something like that."

Her plan was once again melting away. She had to keep things on track. "Maybe you could make an exception this week. I could really use your help."

He shook his head. Still keeping his back to her. "No. My plans can't be changed. I'm not available any Friday night."

The tone of his voice warned her not to pursue the matter, even as her curiosity exploded.

Luke picked up his tool belt. "Tell Camille the lunch was great. Guys will like it."

Sara set her jaw. Could he have been more rude? Just when she thought they were developing a good relationship, he'd gone all iceberg on her again. She'd never met anyone who could go from nice to ice so quickly. What was he hiding? Or was it fear he was shielding himself from? Sara cleared away her food, then closed the container. Why? What had happened to him in the past that left him so skittish?

Back at her workstation, Sara tapped her pencil against the list she'd made of things to do Friday night. Without Luke's help, none of it would get done, and she'd fall behind on her schedule. Maybe she could ask Fred to help. No. He'd mentioned he was going to the coast to visit his daughter.

Luke's abrupt retreat nagged at her mind, escalating her frustration. Eyeing her laptop, she made a quick decision and typed in his name, trying to stifle the warning in the back of her mind that said she was snooping. Her attempt proved futile. Her search turned up thousands of Luke McBrides. It was probably just as well. She didn't need to know any personal details about the carpenter. All that mattered was that he did his job to her satisfaction. The rest was his private affair.

Sara rubbed her temple. She didn't like being sneaky or suspicious, but she'd learned the hard way not to trust what a person told you. There was always something more, something hidden. She had to accept that if the man had secrets, she might never know what they were. After all, she didn't plan on sharing her secret with him.

Closing her laptop, she turned her attention to her next task. She'd give Luke his space and concentrate on her job. There was still had a lot to do. She had to finalize the ad for the newspaper, pick up the new business cards from the printer, organize the door prizes for opening day and, most importantly, find an employee to help in the store. Hopefully, she would have someone trained who could share the load with her sister. Once the twins came Camille would need an assistant.

The thought buoyed her spirits. Then she'd be able to get back to job hunting and finally put Blessing behind her. As she pulled into the drive later, her email tone sounded. Quickly she checked her phone and found two new messages from companies she recognized. A bubble of excitement rose in her chest. This could be it. The answer she'd been praying for. Her hopes were short-lived. Neither company had made an offer.

In the safety of her room, she curled up in the window seat, fighting back tears. She was running out of places to apply. She'd signed up for several job search sites online and called a headhunter friend in Chicago, but there wasn't anything close to the job she once held. Brick-and-mortar opportunities were dwindling.

Her life was at a dead end. Drawing her knees up to her chest, she let the tears fall. What was she going to do now? There were still a few applications out there. She had to hold out hope. In the meantime, her first priority was to get the store open. Once that was accomplished, she could focus on the job hunt.

Sara's car was already parked out back when Luke arrived at the store Friday morning. The woman was nothing if not dedicated. He'd come to the store early this morning hoping to move construction along. The major tasks were complete, and now it was down to tackling the smaller but equally time-consuming jobs like cabinet hardware, backsplash and baseboards. Most importantly, they were right on schedule. That should make her happy.

Despite his good news, his conscience pinged. He regretted refusing to help Sara tonight, but his commitment to the group was too important to ignore. Though, he could have handled his refusal more diplomatically. He had to do something about these knee-jerk reactions to Sara. Maybe he could make it up to her. But how? The one thing she wanted from him was to sell his chairs. He couldn't do that. Maybe he could offer to help at a different time.

He walked through the back door and headed toward the front, stopping in his tracks when he saw Sheriff Hughes standing at the checkout counter, talking to Sara. His blood chilled, and his heartbeat pounded in his ears. Why was he here?

The sheriff glanced up and nodded at him. Luke hoped the smile on the officer's face was a good sign. He joined them at the counter. "Morning."

"McBride. Good to see you again. My cousin is really enjoying those bookcases you built for her."

"Good to hear." Sara gave him a curious glance.

"The sheriff was telling me about furniture that is being given away. He thought we, uh, I might be interested in some of it for the store."

Luke smiled, his tension easing. The man was here to see Sara. Not him.

The officer straightened and rested his hand on his utility belt. "Claude Hill passed away a few months ago, and since he had no children, he left everything to his niece. She's here to settle the estate, and she wants to get the old house empty and on the market, ASAP. She doesn't want to toss some of the better pieces, so she thought you might be able to take them on consignment."

"I'm sure I can. I'd hate for anything to end up at the dump."

Luke chuckled under his breath. "You never met a piece of furniture you didn't like. But do you have room for anything else?" His light and teasing tone earned him a smile.

"I'll find a spot. There's the second floor, which I haven't even worked on yet. I'd like to at least look at the items. When can I go?"

"Well, if you have some time, now. She's wanting to leave Blessing tomorrow. Her place is just on the edge of town. Not far."

Sara looked up at Luke with a question in her eyes. "I'm free," he said.

She smiled and nodded. "Great." She scribbled down the address the sheriff gave her, then shoved the sticky note into her pocket of the denim skirt she was wearing. Luke's mood lightened. Maybe this would make up for his earlier rudeness.

They pulled up in front of the small brick Craftsman home, and Sara let out a soft sigh. "How sweet."

Luke leaned over for a closer look, catching a whiff of her tangy perfume. He had to swallow the lump in his throat before he could speak. "It's in bad shape. Doubt she'll get much for it."

Sara shook her head. "Someone will see the potential and bring it back to life. It's just been ignored and neglected too long."

He thought of his own dilapidated house. He'd ignored and neglected it for the last three years. No doubt Sara would scold him for his lack of attention.

The niece answered the door quickly and introduced herself. "Rhonda Nolan. Thank you for coming so quickly. I'm not sure any of these pieces are worth saving, but I just couldn't bring myself to have them hauled off."

"I understand. I'm Sara Holden and this is Luke McBride."

Rhonda shook his hand, her eyes narrowing slightly. "Have we met?"

Luke's pulse skipped. "I don't think so."

"No, probably not. I've only been here a few weeks and haven't met anyone except for friends of Sheriff Hughes and a few of my uncle's friends at church." She walked to the dining room in the back of the old house.

It didn't take long for Sara to agree to take the four large pieces. The buffet table looked good, but the armoire had a damaged door. Luke felt he could repair it easily. The dining room table was in perfect condition, but the Hoosier cabinet was in bad shape.

After agreeing on a price and making arrangements for pickup, they prepared to leave.

"I can't thank you enough. This is a big load off my mind."

Sara extended her hand to the woman. "Thank you, Miss Nolan. These are going to be a nice addition to the store. I'm sure they'll sell quickly."

Rhonda offered her hand to Luke, frowning. "Are you sure we haven't met before? You look so familiar. I just can't place it."

Luke quickly withdrew his hand as his palms began to sweat. "I just have one of those faces. I'm always reminding people of someone they know."

"You're probably right."

Luke's stomach was twisted in knots by the

time they were on their way back to the store. Sara was chattering about the great deal she'd made and all the ideas she had for displaying each piece.

"How soon can you pick the things up tomorrow?"

"I'll have to get with Fred. Loading is a two-man job. It'll have to be early. We have a game at noon." Luke thought about the four large pieces of furniture. It was doubtful Fred could handle it on his own. Luke was not eager to meet Rhonda Nolan again. Had the woman really recognized him, or did he merely resemble someone she knew? There was a time when everyone had recognized him. He'd been forced to hide in his home to avoid threats and accusations.

Thankfully, Sara talked all the way back to the store, and when they arrived, the health department inspector was leaving and gave them a passing grade. Luke sent up a prayer of thanks for the timing. Now he could get back to work and spend less time with Sara. Maybe he could find someone to help Fred tomorrow. He didn't want to see Rhonda and risk triggering her memory.

Coming out of hiding was proving to be a bad idea. The more he interacted with Sara and the store, the more people he'd meet. People who would ask questions and want his skills. He needed to retreat to the workshop. But he couldn't until the store was completed. Then there was the old furniture she'd just purchased in need of repairs. Everywhere he turned, he was getting sucked deeper into life in Blessing. And Sara.

Funny thing was, he was strangely reluctant to return to his old ways. He wanted to see Camille's store open and filled with customers shopping and eating in the little café. He wanted to see Sara smiling and happy.

But then what? She'd made it clear that once the store was open, she would be moving on. Small-town life wasn't for her. She thrived in the energy and exhilaration of the city. She would never be content in the small confines of Blessing.

And he could never go back to the harshness of the city.

He was beginning to wonder why the Lord had brought Sara into his life in the first place.

Chapter Six

Luke watched Jonah tossing the football up in the air Tuesday evening, his concern growing. It wasn't like Sara to be late picking her son up from practice. He'd sent her a text, but she hadn't responded, which could mean she'd either left her phone somewhere in the store and didn't hear it, or she'd forgotten to charge it. Both events weren't unusual. He hated to take Jonah home without her knowing. If she showed up at the ball field and no one was there he knew she'd panic.

Luke joined the boy on the field and held up his hands for the ball. "I'm still waiting for your mom to get back to me. I'm sure she'll be here soon."

Jonah tossed the football. "She gets busy and forgets things sometimes."

Luke sent the ball back to the boy. "We all do from time to time."

"I wish Rusty had been here instead of going to visit his grandma."

"You and your cousin are good buddies, aren't you?"

"Yes, sir. It's like having a brother. I hate being an only child." He sent the ball through the air again. "Do you have brothers and sisters?"

"A brother. He's older but we had fun together." The thought of Will made him smile. He should give him a call. It had been too long.

Jonah caught the ball but didn't toss it back. He stood staring at the pigskin a moment. "Did you have a dad?"

Luke blinked in surprise. "Yes. I did."

"Was he around all the time?"

Luke considered his response. "Yes. Though he worked a lot." Was the boy feeling the absence of a father figure? He was out of his depth here and had no idea how to navigate this topic.

"My uncle Dave works a lot but he's always home at night."

"He's a good man. And your mom is a good mother, too." He felt the need to champion Sara.

Jonah tossed the ball. "I guess. But she wants

to leave here, and I don't. I keep telling her, but she won't listen."

Luke had stepped into dangerous ground. He couldn't afford to side with Jonah, but he couldn't ignore the boy, either. "Maybe you need to keep trying. She's been very busy with the store. I'm there every day, and I see how hard she works. She's very eager to make your aunt's store a success to thank her for all she's done."

Jonah grimaced and lowered his head. "I know."

The daylight was quickly fading, and Luke decided it best to take Jonah home and soothe Sara's worries later. "Come on, champ. Let's go. You can come home with me until we get hold of your mother." Luke sent another text, then loaded up the equipment and drove out of the lot.

Jonah was quiet on the ride. Maybe he needed some encouragement. "You're a good player. Very fast." The boy's smile made Luke smile, too.

"I like it. It's fun. It's better than art class and music lessons and stuff like that."

"Is that what you did back home?" Apparently Sara's plan for her son didn't include sports.

"Yes, sir. But here I can go outside whenever I want, I can ride a bike and I can explore the woods with Rusty. We found a bunch of old wood for fixing up our clubhouse. We're going to show it to Mr. Fred so he can make us a table. It'll be really cool."

"My brother and I had a secret hideout when we were kids. Our grandpa helped us build it. We spent all our summers in there."

"I don't have a grandpa."

Luke heard the longing and the disappointment in the boy's voice. "But you have Mr. Fred. He's a grandpa, just not your real one."

Jonah smiled. "Yeah, he is. That's cool."

Luke parked the truck, then checked his messages again. Sara still hadn't responded. He was getting worried. Was she all alone in the store? Had something happened? As if on cue, his text alert went off. Sara was on her way.

"Can I see some of your tools?"

"Sure. Your mom's on her way." Luke walked to the workbench where he was assembling another rocker.

"What's this stuff?"

"A rocking chair. Like the one your uncle Dave has."

"The one my mom sits in all the time?"

Jonah frowned. "It doesn't look like a chair. It looks like dumb pieces of wood."

Luke chuckled. "That's how it starts. Now watch. If you set these pieces up like this, and then add boards over the top, it starts to look like a chair."

"Awesome. It's like a puzzle."

"Exactly." Luke was still explaining the process when Sara hurried into the shop.

"I'm so sorry, Jonah. I got caught up in work, and then a woman came by asking about a job. It took longer to interview her than I expected, then I started to show her around and realized my phone was still in the kitchen and I'd missed all my texts." She hugged her son. "How was practice?"

"Good. Mr. Luke is showing me how he puts his rockers together."

"Thank you, Luke, for watching out for him. I forgot Dave and Camille were visiting family this evening and I had to pick up Jonah."

Sara held his gaze, causing his heart to flutter. He liked helping her. He liked her. He was beginning to dread the end of the café project. It would be completed soon, and his skills would no longer be required. She wouldn't need him anymore. The realization shouldn't have stung so deeply. Quickly he turned away, fearful of his emotions being revealed in his expression. "No problem. We had some quality man-to-man time, didn't we, champ?"

Jonah grinned. "Yes, sir, we did."

Sara frowned. "That sounds ominous. Should I be worried?"

"Just guy talk, Mom. Nothing a girl would want to hear."

Luke chuckled and nudged his shoulder. "Right on."

Sara gave them a puzzled shake of her head. "I really appreciate you taking care of my boy."

He wanted to tell her he'd always be there for her, but he doubted it would be received well. Instead, he nodded and tried to keep his expression neutral. "Anytime."

"I'll see you tomorrow, then."

He fought the urge to say, *No. I quit.* Being close to her was taking a toll on his emotions, but he knew he couldn't do that to her. He'd have to see this job through no matter how difficult it became. "Of course." Besides, his time with her was running out, and he wanted as much of that time as possible.

She opened her mouth to speak, but Fred entered the barn at that moment.

"Miss Sara. Hello, Jonah."

"Hi, Mr. Fred."

"Hello, Fred. We were just leaving. Thanks again, Luke."

The door closed behind them, and Fred came toward him, a deep frown on his weathered face. "We need to talk."

"What about?" The look on his friend's face and the ominous tone of his voice caused Luke to study the older man more closely.

"It's Mike, your financial guy. He's gone."

"What do you mean gone?"

"Disappeared along with all your money, and several other people's too. Luke, my boy. I'm afraid you're broke."

Luke smiled. Surly Fred was joking? "That's not funny."

"I'm not joking, friend. I've been on the phone with your bank and Dave. It's not just you. He's stolen money from all his clients."

Luke struggled to understand what Fred was saying. "No. Mike wouldn't do that. We've been friends for years. He's no crook."

Fred held his gaze. "He is now."

Luke set his hands on his hips, mentally digesting this shift in his status. Broke? How was that possible? He'd been set for life. What had caused his friend to undermine him this way?

More importantly, what in the world did he do now?

* * *

Sara stole a glance at Luke as he installed the baseboards in the back of the store. He and Fred had been working hard to get all the details finished for the big opening day. But something had changed with Luke. The last couple of days he'd been super-focused on his work and barely spoken to her. What few conversations they'd shared were abrupt and to the point. Not like his normal, easygoing self. She thought about asking him if everything was okay, but he always looked so intent on his work that she hated to interrupt him.

Try as she might to give Luke his space, she was beside herself with concern, wondering what had suddenly caused him to withdraw again into his shell like a hermit crab. He'd been fine the other evening when she'd picked up Jonah. However, when he'd come to work the next day, he'd been sullen and tight-lipped, with a deep scowl furrowing his brow. His mood showed no signs of improving, which only worried her more.

It had to be something other than her being late picking up Jonah or his being inconvenienced with bringing him home. According to Jonah, they'd had a man-to-man talk, which had elevated Luke to near-hero status. Their conversation had something to do with the secret clubhouse. She massaged her forehead. Another family secret she had to deal with.

It was all too much.

Determined to shove her anxiety over Luke's bad mood to the back of her mind, she channeled all her energy to the store. The final push was on, and she had a million things to do before opening day. There were at least half a dozen vignettes that needed fine-tuning.

Otherwise, things were coming together as planned. The kitchen was gleaming, the walls were painted and all the back rooms looked bright and fresh. Even her new hire, Alice, was rapidly getting up to speed. Alice Bailey was Marilyn Parks's mother and was proving to be a big help. She even knew someone who might want to manage the café. That meant Camille could enjoy the fun part of her store and leave all the details to her employees.

The only thing missing was a new job for herself. She had been contacted about a position in Portland, Maine, but the pay wasn't worth the move across country. It was becoming harder and harder to keep her hopes up. Thankfully, the store kept her too busy to dwell on her unemployment. But what would happen when the store was open and Camille was ready to take over again?

Maybe it was time to look for a different type of job. But what?

Elbows deep in a box of old china later that day, Sara brushed hair off her forehead and glanced down at her phone. Camille. Lately she'd been spending more time on bed rest, so the call sent a jolt of concern through Sara's veins. "Sis. Everything okay?"

"Well, not really."

"What's wrong? Are you all right?"

"I'm fine. I have a problem with an order I placed."

Sara listened while her sister explained about the table and chairs she'd ordered that were now unavailable. "I've been calling around, and I found some up in Tupelo, and the guy gave me a great price. There's only one thing."

Sara didn't have to guess. She knew the way Camille's mind worked. "What?"

"You have to drive up there and pick them up tomorrow or he'll sell them to another customer."

Sara rubbed her forehead. "Sis, I don't have time for that. It'll take nearly the whole day to get up there and back. We open in a couple of days."

"I know. If I was able, Dave and I would get them. I really need these, Sara, or else the café can't open for the festival."

Sara chewed her bottom lip. There was no use arguing. "Fine. Can I use Dave's truck?"

"Oh no. The tables and chairs won't fit in a pickup. I've rented a van. You can pick it up first thing in the morning from Haul-it."

Sara blew out an irritated breath. She didn't need this right now. "Camille, I can't drive a van."

"I know. That's why I thought you could ask Luke to go with you. He's been such a tremendous help and all. And he's such a nice guy."

Sara rolled her eyes. Not this week. He's been a grim, silent and withdrawn guy. "Oh, I don't know, Camille. There's still so much to do here, and we haven't much time left."

"Exactly. There's not much time."

She was trapped. "Fine. I'll talk to him."

Sara mulled over the request. The last thing she wanted to do was spend a long day in an uncomfortable van with a grumpy Luke. Unfortunately, she had no choice. They couldn't open the café without tables and chairs. She glanced toward the back, where the men were finishing. Maybe she could ask Fred to pick up the furniture. She nodded. Yep. Definitely a better idea. She'd speak to Fred the first chance she got. A few minutes later she heard the back door bang shut and hurried to the kitchen only to find Luke alone.

"Where's Fred?"

"Gone."

"Gone where?"

"Mobile."

Sara frowned. "Mobile, Alabama?"

"That's the only one I know." He stopped work and faced her. "Something I can help you with?"

She bit her lip. "When's he coming back?"

"A couple of days."

Another plan dashed. She studied Luke a moment. He looked less sour than he had yesterday. Not that it mattered. She had a job to do. Surely she could endure a trip with Luke for a good cause?

Unless of course, he said no. In that case she had no Plan B.

Luke rested his forearms on the railing of the Blessing Bridge, soaking in the peace and serenity of the surroundings. The history of the bridge was posted at the entrance to the winding trail and told of a mother whose son had polio, and after she prayed at the bridge he recovered. The bridge had become a place to find solitude to lift your prayers to the Lord and receive comfort and reassurance.

The Blessing Bridge and the land had been officially named the Blessing Bridge Prayer Garden, and it lived up to its name. He'd come here this morning looking for courage and direction.

He'd been caught off guard yesterday when Sara had asked him to drive to Tupelo to pick up an order for Camille. The tension between them this week had been fierce, and he was to blame for that. Luke knew his lousy mood had erected a wall between him and Sara. He was still trying to cope with losing his money and coming to grips with the betrayal of a trusted friend.

He'd been on the phone with Dave and the bank, juggling what funds remained. He had to face the fact that from now on he'd have to earn his living, and the obvious path was his woodworking abilities. The monetary loss was demoralizing, but he only had himself to support, and if it came down to it, he could sell the farm. Fred had reminded him that the future wasn't over, just turned in a new direction.

A bird swooped down and landed at the edge of the pond, stretching its wings. Luke smiled at the image. It was a picture of his life right now. He'd landed at the edge of an obstacle, and he had to stretch his wings in a new direction. It wouldn't be the first time.

He closed his eyes and allowed the solitude around him to seep deep inside. Past the anger, below the uncertainty and through the pain to the part of him that found peace. The place where he could hear the Lord's voice.

Today the Lord had reminded him of all the things that had worked out for him when he trusted in the Lord's plan. There was Sara's offer to sell his rockers in her store. Besides, he had a loft full of furniture and material enough to do dozens more. But could he live off his woodworking? Sara thought so. How many times did the Lord need to prove Himself before Luke ceased to have doubts?

Luke turned his steps back toward the parking lot. He'd be okay. He had a lot to be thankful for. The sting of betrayal would ease. The comfort of financial security was nice, but he'd survive without it.

Another reason to be grateful came to mind. Sara.

It was becoming harder to deny his growing attraction. He did his best when at the shop to keep his distance. Not an easy thing to do when she kept asking him to help her move things. Even knowing she would be leaving at some point, he had to admit that meeting her, spending time with her was a blessing. She'd given him a new point of view.

Unfortunately, he wasn't looking forward to the trip to Tupelo. It wasn't just the close proximity with Sara that was unsettling, but also the realization that it was time to tell her about his financial setback. And that opened the door for the topic of his rockers.

All he had to do was set aside his pride and his fear and step out in faith. He'd offer his chairs to Sara and see what happened. It was risky. The attention it might generate was troublesome, but it was either sell the farm or sell his rockers. The hardest part would be eating that big slice of humble pie and telling Sara.

An hour later, he pulled the van to a stop near the back door of the store, gathering his courage. The store would be open in a few days, and if she was to be believed, having one of his rockers would be a boost to her business. That remained to be seen.

As long as it didn't boost his public awareness. This would only work if he could remain out of the spotlight.

* * *

Sara hurried out the back door of the shop the moment the large van came to a stop. He was late. He'd texted that there was a holdup at the rental office, which meant they were already behind schedule and forcing her to shift her plan for the day. Opening day was around the corner, and she resented having to take this time away from the shop.

A rush of shame burned through her veins. Her sister was being so generous offering to let her stay in the house until she found work. All she asked in return was help with her store. If that meant taking a day trip to pick up furniture for the store, then so be it.

She had to remember her sister's needs were her priority now. At least until the babies came and the store was open again.

Still, she wasn't looking forward to this trip. It was going to be awkward and uncomfortable, especially with Luke in a dark mood. It meant he wouldn't be inclined to talk. He was hiding something. He had been from the first day. She couldn't deal with secretive people. She'd had too many secrets in her life—harmful, life-changing ones—and she would not go through that again.

Luke met her at the passenger door. "Good

morning. I brought you a cup of coffee for the ride. Cream, no sugar."

He held out the cup, a smile on his face. She hesitated. "Why?"

Luke frowned. "Because you like coffee, and I figured you'd need some to get the day started."

"Oh. Thanks. I'm just not used to…" How did she explain that people didn't usually do thoughtful things for her? Her husband never had, being more interested in his own needs. Luke, on the other hand, was always kind and considerate. She took the cup and gave him a smile. "And thank you for helping out. Camille sprung this trip on me."

"All part of the job."

"I have so much to do. I really don't have time for this. This has seriously messed up my plans."

"Would you like me to drive up and get it?"

Her mood lifted. It was the perfect solution. She could continue work on the store and Luke could pick up the order. She dismissed the idea instantly. Camille wanted her approval on the furniture. She had an obligation. "That's very nice of you, but I need to handle this for my sister."

Once inside the van, Sara was relieved to

find the seat comfortable and the cab neat and clean. In a small town like Blessing, she'd expected torn plastic seats and bottom-of-the-line interior. However, the space between the seats was narrow and intimate. It would make for a long journey. She'd labeled her growing attraction to Luke as nothing more than curiosity. He was a private man, which made her wonder about him. The problem was, the more she learned about him the more she wanted to know.

They drove in silence while Luke navigated the highway out of Blessing and up through Meridian. When the silence dragged on, she searched for a topic of conversation, but Luke beat her to it.

"What is it with you and making plans? Do you have a plan for everything?"

Not a topic she would have chosen. "Yes. Actually. I think everyone should have backup plans." She kept her gaze forward, but she sensed his scrutiny.

"Does this have anything to do with your aversion to surprises and secrets?"

She looked out the passenger window, debating whether to answer him. It was never easy to talk about herself, but Luke had shown her a kindness by bringing coffee. "My dad lost his job, but he didn't tell my mom for two months. He kept it secret until it was too late. By the time he told us we'd lost our house and had to move into a small apartment. If he'd told us sooner, we might have been able to fix things." She met his gaze and saw understanding in his blue eyes.

"How old were you?"

"Twelve. I just couldn't understand why the grown-ups didn't have a plan in place to take care of things. They were supposed to protect us. It seemed so irresponsible."

"So that's when you decided to plan out your life. How did that work out for you?"

"Fine, most of the time." Planning had prepared her for what was around the corner.

"I'm not sure everything in life can be prepared for. It's too unpredictable."

"It doesn't hurt to plan ahead." Especially because life was unpredictable.

"No. It doesn't. Especially for a single mom. It must be hard juggling all your responsibilities. Planning would make sense."

No one had ever understood her situation or her need to be prepared at all times. Camille was always telling her to stop worrying, to just let things work themselves out. Sara couldn't live that way. She had to wonder what had happened in Luke's life that he understood. She glanced over at him, noticing that the pale green-and-blue button-down shirt and faded jeans softened the dark brown of his hair.

"I guess your plans since coming to Blessing haven't always worked out," he offered.

He had no idea. "No. I spend most of my time drawing up new plans."

"Maybe you're overthinking things. An overall plan is great but micromanaging can backfire." He looked at her and made a circling gesture around his temple with his finger. "It'll make you crazy."

It was on the tip of her tongue to explain how it was the details that made a plan work, but she shook her head. "Success is in the details."

"Perhaps. Have all your plans worked out to your liking?"

Luke had a way of cutting to the chase of things. He'd hit the core of her struggle since coming to Blessing. "No. But that doesn't mean I stop planning."

"Maybe not, but you might try leaving a little room for the unexpected. Let the surprises rock your boat but not capsize it."

"Is that what happened to you? Your life got capsized?"

He was silent a moment. "Isn't everyone's life capsized at some point or another?"

She trained her gaze out the window. Hers had hit the rocks twice in her lifetime. "Yes. I suppose it does." She gave Luke a quick smile, and he returned it, making her pulse jump oddly.

"The store is looking good. You've done an amazing job. You're a very talented lady."

"Thank you." The compliment made her smile, but something behind his tone drew her attention. His hands were gripping the steering wheel more tightly than necessary, and there was obvious tension in his broad shoulders. What was going on behind those ice blue eyes?

"Do you think your special round table will lure in customers?"

It was an odd question for him to ask. She tensed. What was he getting ready to tell her? "I do. It's gorgeous. I'd love to sell it the first day we're open." Luke glanced out the side window briefly, then fell silent for a long moment.

"Would a rocking chair or two help?"

Sara jerked her head to look at him. Was he serious? Luke kept his gaze on the road ahead. The only indication she had of his mood was the rapid flexing of his jaw. Anticipation raced through her veins. Was it possible he'd changed his mind? "Have you decided to place your rocker in the store?"

"Maybe."

"Luke, that would be wonderful. I know I can sell them for top dollar, and they'd really add a special attraction." She studied him a moment. "What happened? You were adamant that you would never sell your furniture."

Luke shrugged as if searching for the right words. He stared at his hands a long moment before answering. "It seems that the person I entrusted with my financial future has robbed me blind."

She took a moment to process what he'd said. "Oh, Luke. That's awful. I'm so sorry." She reached over and squeezed his arm. "Did you have any idea what he was doing?"

"No. Neither did the other people he ruined. He was a close friend. He'd helped me through a really tough time and made sure I was financially secure."

"What does this mean?"

He glanced at her briefly. "It means I have to earn a living now. My woodworking is no longer a pastime I enjoy, but my sole means of support."

Everything came into focus. Luke's life had

been capsized. She understood that all too well. She also understood how difficult it must have been for him to admit defeat and agree to her idea for selling his furniture. "Such as placing your chairs in the store to sell?"

"If you're still willing."

She smiled as her spirits soared. "Of course. They are the perfect piece for the store. I'll do all I can to market them and make you a huge success."

Luke winced. "Let's just put one in the store and see how it goes. Though you did promise I'd make a fortune."

She giggled, relieved to hear the teasing tone back in his voice. "Did I say that? You must have misunderstood."

He shook his head and grinned. "Women. Always making promises."

"Luke, I'm really sorry for what you're going through. I can understand. I felt the same way when my job was eliminated. My normal life was gone. Finding another job is proving difficult. Thankfully, Camille was literally the answer to my prayers. I never bought into that close-a-door-open-a-window point of view, but I do now." She squeezed his arm again, and he captured her gaze, his blue eyes warm and tender. She wanted to encourage him. "Maybe I'm your open window."

Luke looked at her with a surprised expression, and she realized how her comment must have sounded. "I mean, you know, your new future. This is a new opportunity. A partnership."

The more she said the worse the whole idea sounded.

It hit her then that if this arrangement happened, she'd be working with Luke more closely than ever. The idea should have alarmed her, but instead, a swell of excitement chased through her veins. He'd done so much for her with the remodel and now was her chance to help him by giving him a new career.

"You might be right." He reached over and took her hand. The contact filled her with warm contentment. "Guess we'll see soon enough."

She met his gaze, and the affection reflected in his eyes sent her heart pounding. Did he have feelings for her, or was she merely indulging in wishful thinking? The grip of his hand said he did. Did she want him to care? She had no answer. Her life was too unsettled now, too capsized.

He released her hand, and she inhaled a

breath and turned her thoughts to the rockers and how she would utilize them in her sister's store. That was a much safer problem for her mind to focus on than her confusing feelings about Luke.

Correction. She had no feelings about Luke. Did she?

Chapter Seven

Luke unhooked the strap holding the rocker securely in the back of his truck, then removed the cloth cover. Today was a day he'd never expected to face. He was putting one of his rockers on sale. Part of him wanted to take the thing back home, but he didn't have a choice any longer. He had to make a living, and this was the first step. He had serious doubts that he could support himself solely on his carpentry skills, but Sara was convinced.

Their trip to Tupelo yesterday had been enlightening. Not only had the café tables and chairs proved to be the perfect complement for the store, but his relationship with Sara had taken a new and pleasing turn. After picking up the furniture they'd stopped for a bite to eat. He'd steered the conversation toward her and let her regale him with tales of her and Camille growing up. The three-hour trip back to Blessing had flown by.

His concern over Sara's reaction to his poverty had been unwarranted. He'd worried what she would think. Although he wasn't sure why, he didn't want to look weak in her eyes. He felt like a failure in his own mind, but Sara had been kind and compassionate. And understanding.

He couldn't forget that awkward moment when she spoke about windows being opened and her being his open window. The air between them had been thick with tension. He'd been aware of every small detail of her pretty face and of his attraction to her. He'd found himself following that line of thought over and over all night. Somehow, little by little, she'd pried open his tightly sealed door and let the light shine into his dim world.

Was Sara a new start for him? He had been thinking about his future lately. What if he had a chance for a full life, a family, a woman to share his dreams? But it was hard to share when the person wasn't around, and Sara had her mind set on getting back to the big city.

Lifting the rocker from the truck bed, he carried it inside. Offering his work for sale was a big step toward changing his life. He had second thoughts, third and fourth thoughts, but he was devoid of options. All he could do was pray that selling his chairs would solve his problems and keep the old ones from cropping up again.

Luke set the chair in the first open space he found. Sara probably had a special spot all picked out. She was at the checkout, leaning over one of her plans. He started toward her but stopped when she placed her palms against her cheeks. It was a gesture he'd come to recognize that signaled another job rejection. He wanted to give her a hug, but he doubted she'd welcome the intrusion. Secretly, he was always relieved when her plan had been stymied. He wasn't ready for her to leave.

She looked up and saw him, a big smile replacing the disappointment in her brown eyes.

"It's here." She hurried forward and stroked the back of the chair. "It's gorgeous. Thank you. This is going to be huge for the store."

He hoped not too huge. That wasn't his goal. "Where do you want it?"

Sara motioned for him to follow her to an area near the front window that had been cleared of items. He set the rocker on top of a round braided rug then stood back and watched as Sara gathered items from here and there. Within moments the scene had been set. A galvanized container had been placed beside the rocker and filled with dried flowers. A small, weathered table was positioned on the other side, covered by a crocheted doily topped with a colorful teapot, cup and saucer and an open book. The final touch was a natural color blanket tossed over the back of the chair, which made its walnut stain vibrant. A little pillow with a star in the middle completed the display.

Luke smiled. The vignette looked so inviting he almost wanted to sit down and read the book himself. Maybe Sara was right. Someone might actually want one of his rockers. He set his hands on his hips and shook his head. "Your display makes me want to buy the dumb chair myself."

Sara giggled and leaned toward him. "I won't be surprised if it sells within the first hour I'm open."

Luke chuckled. "I like your optimism."

"I'm so happy."

"You're just saying that because you got what you wanted."

Sara grinned and tilted her head. "I knew you'd cave sooner or later. You couldn't resist my charm."

His eyes locked with hers, causing his pulse to rev like a high-powered car engine. She was absolutely correct. He was having trouble resisting her sweet charm. He swallowed, then cleared his throat. Sara broke eye contact.

"I can't believe I'm the sole vendor for the McBride Rocker."

"You're not going to make me stand there and tell people about it, are you? Cause that's not happening."

"No. That would be awkward for the customers." She patted his shoulder. "You can stay home in your little workshop. I'll just bring you the money as it comes in."

Luke chuckled. "I can live with that. If you need to borrow my truck to haul all that loot to my house, just let me know."

Sara laughed out loud. Luke realized it was the first time he'd heard her do that. It was a captivating sound, and he wanted to hear it more often.

Fred called from the back. "Can someone lend me a hand here?"

Luke pulled his gaze from Sara and strode to his friend, following him out to his truck. He stared at the odd cabinet sitting in the truck bed. "What's this?"

Fred chuckled. "My project for Sara."

After loading the hutch onto the dolly, they rolled it inside. Sara hurried toward them, a huge grin on her face. "You've finished the hutch."

Fred puffed out his chest. "I think it turned out pretty well, if I say so myself."

"It's adorable. I love it. It's exactly as I envisioned it. Only better."

Fred smiled. "Glad you think so."

Luke watched as Sara examined every aspect of the piece. He struggled to understand why she was so delighted. To him it looked like a hodgepodge of random sections glued together. The upper section with its three shelves had been repaired but maintained its original Parisian green color. The lower section had been the most damaged. Now its counter and backsplash were covered in antique tiles, their green-and-blue pattern complementing the old green paint. The base, with its broken doors and rotted side panel, had been rebuilt and painted a weathered blue. The two metal grilles had been inlaid into the new cabinet doors.

Sara stepped back and smiled, her hands clasped at her chest. "It's the perfect blend of old and new." She wrapped the older man in a big hug. "You're amazing. Thank you. My customers are going to love this. You may have to build a few more."

"I like that idea. We can repurpose all the odds and ends. Sounds like fun."

Sara nodded. "Our own line of furniture. We'll call it Odds and Ends Decor."

Luke rolled the dolly back to the storage room, a strange heaviness forming in his gut. He tried to ignore it, but it sat in his chest like a lump of mud. He'd felt certain Sara would be disappointed with the hutch. Instead, she and Fred had been thrilled by the end product.

What was it they saw that he was missing? Was Sara right? Did he lack imagination? Or was he too stuck in his own point of view to appreciate something that didn't fit into his narrow world?

He took pride in his ability to repair an old piece of furniture and make it look like new. He had received glowing thanks from his customers. But the hutch's appeal escaped him. What about it had brought such joy and appreciation to Sara's face? She'd looked like a little girl who'd been given her heart's desire. Fred had caused that reaction. Luke wanted to be the one to light up her eyes and to bring out that childish delight.

The thought rocked him. He couldn't be falling for her. He couldn't afford to, emotionally, especially since she was leaving. It was a lose-lose situation. He looked over at her to find her staring back at him. His throat tightened at the sight of her sweet smile. She waved, giving him the thumbs-up sign. He nodded, unable to breathe at the sight of her loveliness.

God help him. He would not fall in love with Sara Holden, no matter how tempting the notion. He turned and walked out.

Best to stick to his original idea and keep his distance from Sara.

But how did he do that when all he wanted was to be at her side?

Sara poured herself a glass of sweet tea and took a seat at the kitchen island just as her sister entered.

"You look tired. Busy day?"

Sara nodded. "But a good one. I told you I hired Marilyn Park's mom, Alice Bailey, to manage the store after I'm gone. She worked for the previous owner, and she's going to be a real blessing for you. And she knows someone who might be interested in managing the café when necessary. It's all coming together like I planned."

"We are the champions. We are the champions."

Sara chuckled as Jonah and Rusty marched through the kitchen chanting and raising their fists in the air. They'd won their last game over the weekend, earning the flag football championship. They were looking forward to the team dinner and receiving their trophies.

Camille smiled and waved them away. "Take it outside, fellas. I need peace and quiet, remember?"

The boys scurried out the back door, and Camille eased herself into the rocker, which they had moved into the kitchen so she could feel like part of the family. She sighed and closed her eyes as she gently rocked backward. "This chair is almost as comfortable as my bed."

"I know. It's really amazing. I'm sure it'll sell the moment we open."

"Luke must be excited."

"Actually, he's not been very enthused at all. I can't figure him out."

"What's to figure? He's a great guy."

"Yes, but he's secretive, too."

Her sister gave her a curious look. "What are you talking about?"

"You know, the way he won't talk about himself much and his odd reactions to things. Then there's his reluctance to sell his furniture. Something isn't right with him."

Camille frowned and stopped rocking. "I don't agree at all. Luke is an open book. You really need to stop being so suspicious of everything. You've been this way since you were a kid, and I never understood it."

Sara stifled the sharp retort on the tip of her tongue. How typical of her sister to be too caught up in herself to see someone else's point of view. Sara tried to keep the irritation from her tone when she spoke. "Really? If you recall, my husband had a secret life for years, and you're puzzled by my suspicious nature?"

"Okay, I'll give you that, but still, I thought you said things went really well between you and Luke on the trip the other day."

"They did." Much better than she'd anticipated. Though she ached for his financial situation. She had firsthand experience with losing your income. Still, she was excited about having his furniture for sale in the store. She had no doubt he could make a nice living from his woodworking.

His comment about making a truckload of loot made her smile. She'd come to enjoy his teasing. It had irritated her at first. She'd thought he was being flippant and judgmental, but she'd soon realized he was trying to put her at ease. Luke was always doing nice things for her like bringing her coffee in the morning, and sometimes surprising her with sweets from Blair's Bakery. He even complimented her on her wardrobe on a regular basis. It made her happy that he noticed what she wore. As a result, she'd started taking more care when dressing in the morning.

Initially she'd been suspicious of his motives. Her husband had only made kind gestures when he was preparing to disappear for weeks at a time. Luke was different. Yet his wall of secrecy was still a large, flashing danger sign complete with skull and crossbones. Her instincts kept telling her there was more to him, something good, but she couldn't get past the protective barrier he always wore. Why? What was he hiding from? What didn't he want the world to know about Luke McBride?

Sara took a sip of her tea and pulled her attention back to her sister. "He was very nice on the trip, and he even opened up a bit." She chose not to share Luke's financial problem with Camille. She felt certain he wouldn't like that news to get out.

"Well, I think he's a real catch. You only have to watch him with the team to know he's a good guy. I only saw the games on video, but it was obvious. I know that no good husband of yours, Elliot, did a number on you, but you need to stop looking for secrets behind everyone."

Sara's old wounds reopened, raising her defenses. "What about Dad's secrets?"

"What secrets?"

"That he'd lost his job and didn't tell us until it was too late, and we lost the house and had to live in that horrible little apartment forever."

Camille studied her closely, a puzzled look on her face. "Sis, he didn't keep that secret. I knew. Mom knew. I guess they thought you were too young to understand. And it wasn't a horrible place. It was nice. We were only there a year or so, then we got another house. That cute little cottage on Langford Drive."

Sara searched her memory. Her recollections didn't match with her sister's. But then there was six year difference in their ages. Camille would have been a teenager when their dad lost his job. She had a different perspective. All Sara could dig up was a vague picture of a brick house.

"Is that why you became so controlling?" Camille asked.

Sara bristled. "I'm not. I just think people should be open and not keep things secret, that's all. Secrets can destroy lives."

Camille inhaled a slow breath. "Oh my. I should have made the connection. I'm so sorry. I never understood why you suddenly became so obsessed with your plans. You used to be so carefree. Elliot's secret life must have made you even more leery of people and their motives."

Sara's eyes grew moist. It meant the world to her to know her sister understood. "How can I ever trust again after what Elliot did?"

"I know. But you can't live your life this way. It's not healthy for you or Jonah. You have to find a way to turn that over to the Lord and let Him help you through. You're stuck in an emotional crevasse, and you have to climb out and move on. Maybe that's why you're here with us. To change the direction of your life."

Sara held her tongue. This new direction was only a temporary detour. *Her* new direction was the road back to the city. There was nothing long-term here for her or Jonah.

So why did an image of Luke suddenly fill her thoughts?

Luke attached the lock to the small wooden box, then set it aside. He'd been edgy and restless today. Visions of Sara's smile, her obvious connection to Fred, still left a hollow feeling in the center of his chest that refused to dissipate. He'd tried to work, but he didn't have the concentration to tackle a real project, so he'd put together a treasure box for Jonah and Rusty to have in their secret clubhouse. Fred had helped the boys turn the old shed into a sweet little hideout. They'd been spending time after school and on weekends fine-tuning their space. The treasure box was Luke's contribution.

Tucking the gift under his arm, he started across the drive and around the back of the barn until he came to the old fence rails and the silo where the shed was situated. He ducked inside and placed the box on the small table, causing it to wobble. Glancing around, he smiled. It was nicer than the clubhouse he and his brother had made. He knew the boys would have hours of fun here.

Suddenly tired, he eased onto the bench, rubbing his forehead. Seeing his rocker displayed in the shop, recalling the joy on Sara's face, had left him with a wave of doubts. Had he made a mistake in agreeing to sell his chairs? He'd second-guessed his decision a dozen times.

Sara was convinced the rockers would bring a good price, and she was overjoyed to have them in the store. She believed in him and was convinced his rocker would sell quickly. Did he want them to? What would happen after the sale? Would the new owner want to meet him? Want to know about him? It would start innocently enough. Simple curiosity about the craftsman, but one internet search could lead to another, and then what?

But what if the chairs didn't sell? He needed to earn a living. He clasped his hands behind his head and stared upward. He didn't know which scenario was more frightening: to see his chairs become a success or discover that no one wanted what he'd made.

A light tapping sound on the clubhouse door caught his attention. Fred peeked in. "I had a feeling I'd find you here."

"Really? Why's that?"

"It's the most private place on the farm short of the hayloft, which is packed with furniture." Fred pulled up a campstool. "So, what's eating at you, son? You have the look of a man pulled in two directions."

Luke took a moment to sort through his thoughts. "I'm not sure agreeing to sell my rockers in the store was such a good idea."

"Why's that?"

Luke shrugged. "Who knows where it will lead?"

"Maybe to something wonderful. You're a talented craftsman. Your work should be celebrated."

"My work, yes. Me, not so much."

Fred scowled and pointed a finger at Luke's face. "You have to stop trying to protect yourself from any kind of attention. You keep your guard up so high no one can get close to you that way. If you continue like this you'll always be alone. Is that what you want?"

"I'm trying to protect others from being put in an awkward position."

His friend grunted in disgust. "Nonsense."

Luke shook his head. "My past is like an oil spill covering everyone who learns of it, tainting their point of view, shifting their opinion of me and leaving behind a thick residue of doubt that would never completely disappear."

Fred scowled. "That's malarkey. Your past is just a bump in your life. The only one stuck in the residue is you. Have you told Sara about your oil spill?"

Luke glared at his friend. Sometimes Fred overstepped his role as friend and farm manager. "No."

Fred leaned forward, his gaze intent. "While we're on the subject, how do you feel about the lovely Sara?"

"I don't know what you mean."

Fred shook his head and pushed himself up from the stool. "Boy, you are more out of touch with things than I ever imagined. I know a man in love when I see one. Go take a good look at yourself in a mirror." Fred left, letting the door slam behind him.

Luke clasped his hands in front of his chin. The older man had a point. Sooner or later she'd learn the truth about his past. That was why he couldn't let things get out of hand. Having his life exposed to the public to dissect and devour had been a horror he wouldn't wish on anyone. Let alone someone he loved.

Fred was right about that, too.

He was fairly sure he'd fallen for Sara Holden.

Sara mulled over her conversation with her sister throughout the next day despite the hectic pace at the store. The opening was this weekend, and everyone was working feverishly to get ready. Luke and Fred were taking care of all the little details with the remodel while she was busy training Alice on the register and handling merchandise. Edith Pugh had come on board to manage the café, and she and Camille were texting about the menu.

Camille was thrilled to be able to participate. The inactivity wore her down at times.

Despite her busyness, Sara couldn't keep thoughts of Luke out of her mind. By the end of the day, she was anxious to get back to the farmhouse and relax. Her nerves were frayed. She'd been questioning decisions about the layout, the décor, the marketing. So much rested on this opening. She'd promised her sister she'd turn her business around. What if she got it all wrong? What if no one came? What if no one bought anything?

And what about Luke? She'd promised him his rockers would sell and provide him a living wage. But she didn't know that for certain. What if she let both of them down?

Parking her car near the house, she got out, anxiety coursing along her veins. Maybe a brisk walk down the long drive to the mailbox would work off some of her stress. A large stack of envelopes rested inside the white country-style receptacle. She sorted through them, slipping her mail into her jacket pocket. The thick envelope at the bottom of the stack caught her attention. It wasn't addressed to her or her sister. The name printed on the paper was Lucian McBride. The return address was from Chicago. Was that where Luke was from?

Luke? Obviously, the mailman had left it by mistake. But the name was wrong. Was Luke really Lucian? Why would he change his name? Her defenses and her suspicions shot into high gear. Had she been right all along and did Luke have something to hide?

Her stomach knotted. She couldn't go through this again. Was she doomed to have people lie to her all her life?

Not this time. Never again.

Sara hurried back to the house and up to her room, grateful that the boys were in the bonus room playing video games and Camille was resting.

Opening up her computer, she typed in the name Lucian McBride, Chicago, and gasped when a long string of hits appeared. She scanned the first one and caught her breath. Lucian McBride convicted of murdering his wife.

His blood chilled. Luke a murderer? No. That wasn't possible. Or was it? She would never have believed her husband would betray her the way he had. Anything was possible.

Only one way to find out. She clicked on the first link and started to read. After scanning the first five options Sara leaned back in her chair, her eyes moist. Her initial horror and doubts had turned to sadness and compassion.

Luke was innocent. He'd been convicted of killing his wife but acquitted when the real killer had come forward and confessed. He'd gone through an arrest, a trial and a conviction. Only to be exonerated and set free. The case had created a media frenzy in Chicago.

She couldn't imagine a man like Luke having to suffer such an ordeal. No wonder he was so protective. So closed and isolated. Now she understood his aversion to having his photo taken and his abrupt shutdown when pushed about his past. Her heart ached for him. How hard it must have been to endure such a scandal. She knew a little about public humiliation. That crippling feeling that the world was staring at you, condemning you. Her solution had been to hide in her work. Luke must have done the same thing.

Closing the computer, Sara checked her watch. Luke should be home now. She had to see him and let him know she understood, and that he had a friend in her. She would keep his secret. She was on his side.

Taking the backstairs, she made her way quietly out of the house and hurried across the lawn to the narrow path that led between the trees that opened out on Luke's property. Dusk was settling over the sky, casting an eerie spookiness to the old Victorian house. A light in the front window encouraged her, but when she stood at the door, knuckles ready to tap on the old wood, her courage sagged.

Maybe this wasn't such a good idea. He'd made it clear he liked his privacy, and now she knew why. She should let sleeping dogs lie, but her heart wanted him to be free from the fear and condemnation and live his life again. She understood how important that was. What would she say? How would she start? Would he be angry and order her out of his life?

The door suddenly opened, drawing a gasp from her throat. Luke stood there, a frown on his chiseled features. "Is everything okay? Jonah? Camille?"

Sara breathed a sigh of relief. He was concerned, not angry. But how long would that last once she told him what she'd discovered? "Everyone is fine. But we need to talk."

Chapter Eight

Luke's heart was pounding. What could bring Sara to his door at this hour? She never came to his house, and the look on her face revealed her distress. But if it wasn't Jonah or Camille, what did she need to talk about? Something at the store? He shook himself mentally, stepping aside and allowing her to enter. "All right." He led the way to the parlor, the only room with seating. She stepped inside and froze. Heat warmed his cheeks. It was a college kid's idea of home. What must Sara be thinking?

He forced a smile and gestured for her to sit in the recliner, then hurried to the kitchen to retrieve one of the small wooden chairs that he'd found in the old pantry.

He tried to make his voice calm yet curious. "What's going on? Something wrong at the store?"

She shook her head, biting her lip. Her hands were clasped tightly in her lap, and the look of discomfort on her face had deepened. He braced himself. Whatever it was, he'd try to help her.

She held his gaze a long moment, then reached into her jacket pocket and pulled out a large envelope, scanning the address slowly before handing it to him. The moment he saw his name, Lucian McBride, printed on the envelope he knew his world was about to come crashing down around his ears.

"This was left in Camille's mailbox by mistake."

He took the envelope, his shoulders stiffening. "I see."

"I looked up the name and…"

"You found out who I am." Luke stood and moved off a few paces.

"I already knew who you were. I just discovered what happened to you."

Luke faced her, every muscle in his body tensed. "And you've come to tell me to get lost. Can't have a convicted killer around your son."

Sara stood and faced him, her expression filled with compassion. "No. I know the truth. I came to tell you I understand."

Luke exhaled a skeptical huff. "No one understands."

"Oh, but I do. I've had my run-in with public humiliation. The shame, the stares and the accusations from strangers."

Luke shook his head. It was sweet of her to offer comfort, but she had no idea what he'd been through. "Not possible."

"Oh, it's very possible."

He held her gaze. Her tone had a ring of sincerity in it, of experience. Did she really get what he'd undergone? "What happened? How can you know what it was like for me?"

She waved off the question. "It doesn't matter. I want to talk about you."

Luke turned away. Now he saw it. She might sympathize, but that didn't change his past. Might as well bow out gracefully. "I'll see that Fred finishes the store for you."

"I don't want him. I want you."

"Then what do you want from me?" Surely she had a request? He'd learned that everyone wanted something.

"I want to know about you. What happened? How did you get here? Why are you hiding when you were proven innocent?"

Luke huffed. "Why? So you can share the juicy story, satisfy the curiosity of everyone in Blessing?"

Her warm brown eyes turned stormy, and

for a moment he thought she might slap him. "I want to know because I care about you. We're friends. Good friends."

He wanted to believe her and the sincerity he saw in her eyes, but he'd been stung too many times. He took a deep breath and set his hands on his hips. He needed a moment to collect himself. "Are you thirsty? I have some sweet tea."

Sara studied him a moment. "Sure."

He poured two glasses, taking the opportunity to gather his courage. He'd worked with Sara long enough to know she wasn't the vindictive type nor one to spread idle gossip. Besides, he knew this day would come sooner or later. Might as well deal with it here and now. He handed her a glass and sat down. "Where do you want me to start?"

"Wherever you're comfortable."

Sara waited patiently for him to begin. There was no judgment in her attitude, only an easy silence. He took a deep breath and began. She listened as he explained his difficult marriage. Both career-minded and working long hours. Then his wife's sudden desire to start a family, but the timing all wrong. He'd been chosen as one of the promising young engineers in the city. His picture was on the cover of an industry magazine. She had started demanding more of his attention and started to drink heavily. They argued constantly. Police were called one night when she broke a lamp against the wall.

Luke stared into the distance, rubbing his bottom lip, afraid to look at the condemnation in Sara's eyes. "A few weeks later, I came home to find her stabbed to death. I couldn't believe what I was seeing. I thought maybe it wasn't too late, so I pulled the knife out."

"Oh, Luke, no. Why did you do that?"

"All I could think of was that I had to get that thing out of her." He clasped his fists under his chin. "It was stupid, I know. Someone had called the police, and there I was. Holding the weapon." He stole a glance at Sara. Her eyes were filled with gentleness. At least she didn't hate him. Yet.

"The rest is all a blur. I only remember bits and pieces. I had the best lawyer in town, but the case hit a note with the public. The press built it up. Rising star, wanting to dump a spouse who was holding him back. Every day the tide turned more against me. The public started to draw up sides. During the trial they gathered outside the courthouse, yelling, calling for my head. Reporters and cameras were in my face every moment. I was the lead topic on the evening news every day."

"Were there no friends to stand up for you?"

Luke shook his head. "I was never good at making friends. I only had time for my career. My lifestyle worked against me. I couldn't prove where I was that night, and I'd had a huge fight with her that morning."

He paced off a few steps. "The trial is a blur. I only remember parts of it. The verdict came, and I was too worn down to even react. The next thing I remember is being hauled off to prison."

"Did you appeal?"

"My attorney was working on it, but I felt he was dragging his feet. He'd been a friend of my wife's. Not mine."

"How long were you incarcerated?"

"Nearly nine months. Then one day my attorney told me someone had come forward and confessed to the killing."

"Who?"

Luke rubbed his chin. "My wife's lover. He'd been pushing her to leave me, but she wasn't ready."

"Why did he suddenly confess?"

Luke looked into Sara's eyes. The tenderness he saw there and the soothing tone of her voice bolstered his courage. It felt good, very good, to share his story with someone. With Sara. "I didn't ask. Didn't care. I walked out of prison, bought this farm and started a new life."

"With a new name?"

Luke shrugged. "A small change."

"So you started building as a way to heal?"

"As a way to keep busy and not think. To keep away from people who might recognize me. I couldn't go through that again." He looked at her. What was it about this woman that made him feel safe to bare his soul? "It was like walking naked through the world every day. The stares, the taunts, the accusations left me feeling as if I'd been skinned raw. I couldn't endure that again."

Sara nodded and lightly touched his knee. "Oh, I see. When you found out I lived in Chicago you were afraid I might recognize you."

"Yes. I didn't want to run the risk of someone remembering me and the trial. It was safer to keep to myself."

"But what about the ball team and the projects you've done around town?"

"Fred has been after me to stop living like I'm guilty. I knew he was right, but it wasn't as easy as it sounds. I started with church. Pastor Miller was a huge help. He's the one who convinced me to coach the team. It took a lot of pushing, but I finally gave in. And I'm glad I did. It gave me a new focus."

"Thank you for sharing what you've been through."

She reached over and took his hand. His fingers curled possessively around hers. He was surprised at how comfortable it felt.

"I never thought I'd tell anyone other than Fred about my past. Especially you."

"Why me?"

"I know how much you hate secrets."

She bowed her head. "I'm sorry, Luke. I made such a big deal about hating secrets that I'd made it impossible for you to confide in me. I've come to realize that everyone has secrets."

"Even you?" She bit her lip. He suspected she had something to share but was hesitant.

"Maybe."

"I hope one day you'll trust me with them. One friend to another." He pulled her to her feet, bringing her close. Looking into her fawn-colored eyes gave him strength and made him feel as if he could accomplish anything with her support. Was it possible that he'd found someone who could take him as he was, past and all?

Sara was unlike anyone he'd ever met. She smiled, and a fierce tension erupted between them. He recognized the affection in her eyes. There was no denying they were drawn to each other. He felt certain that if he kissed her now, she'd respond willingly. He reached out and gently touched her cheek. It was silky soft, and he wanted to slip his hand behind her head and pull her close. Common sense prevailed, and he lowered his hand and inhaled a shaky breath.

He could no longer deny the growing attraction between them. He needed to put a stop to it. Sara might be understanding about his past, but that didn't mean she'd be open to a relationship. But then again, neither was he. He could never let anyone get that close. There was always the risk of someone, even someone close to him, using his past against him for their own end. The way Mike had done.

Sara broke eye contact and stepped away, her gaze taking in the large, sparse room. "This is a wonderful old house. What are your plans?"

He wasn't fooled. He'd seen the blush in her cheeks. Her voice was raspy. She was attempting to divert the uncomfortable air between them. He was grateful. Kissing Sara now would have muddied the situation, possibly destroyed it. The house was a safe topic that would allow them to regain their footing. He had to clear his throat before he could speak. "Total restoration. Eventually. Would you like a tour?"

"Yes. Please."

Her smile sent tingles along his veins. "Where would you like to start?"

She thought a moment. "Let's start at the top and work our way down."

Sara took her time climbing the broad staircase, her fingers trailing along the gracefully carved handrail. At the landing she exhaled an appreciative breath as she took in the large stained glass window.

"This is exquisite. Is it Tiffany?"

"Not sure. Fred thinks it might be, but I'm going to have it evaluated."

They stopped at the top of the stairs, and Sara looked back down. "May I ask why you haven't started working on the house?"

He had no ready answer. "I don't know. I suppose I've been focused on the workshop."

Sara studied him a long moment, then smiled. "Maybe you aren't ready to have a home."

A warm twinge of awareness stirred in the

center of his chest, like a spring thaw. Sara could make this old house a home. One that a man would never want to leave as long as she was inside.

Luke gave her free rein as she wandered from room to room, admiring the elaborate woodwork and stately fireplaces. With each room, her enthusiasm grew. She had ideas for all of them. She instantly knew what colors should be used, the furniture choices and their placement.

Sara saw visions where he only saw the work required.

The tour ended back in the foyer. Sara smiled at him. "Thank you for showing me your home. It's going to be spectacular when it's restored."

Sara's eyes held his, piercing his shield, probing into his psyche. He wanted to break his gaze from hers but couldn't. What was she looking for? What did she see?

The moment seemed to go on forever as they stood there, drawn together by an emotional cord of interest and appreciation. He inhaled a light floral scent that seeped down into his senses. The light in her eyes darkened, and her lips parted slightly before she blinked and turned aside, breaking the bond.

She walked to the front door, stepped outside and turned to face him, a sweet smile on her face.

"Good night, Luke."

As she moved away a jab of fear lanced through him. He'd bared his soul to the core. Where did that leave them? "Sara, it's dark. I'll walk you back."

"All right."

They strolled in silence across his front yard toward the tree line and the narrow path that led to Camille and Dave's property. When they reached the end of the path Luke knew he had to speak up. "Sara, what now? I mean, what will you do with what I told you?" He hated himself for asking. He wanted to take her at her word that she would honor his trust.

"Nothing, Luke. I'll keep it to myself. I wouldn't hurt you that way."

"Does this change things between us?"

"I'm afraid it does." Impish smile.

Luke held his breath. Had he made a big mistake? Let his emotions get the best of his better judgment?

"My admiration and my affection have grown." She laid her palm against his cheek. "I keep my promises, Luke. Especially to my close friends."

He covered her hand with his, the warmth of her touch swirling through his being.

The pull to kiss her, to hold her close and draw comfort from her sweetness was more than he could stand. He leaned forward, lowering his head, his gaze riveted on her lips. A bird screeched overhead. Sara pulled back. "I'll see you at the store in the morning."

Luke watched her until she disappeared into the house, his emotions oscillating between regret for not kissing her and relief that he hadn't overstepped. They'd reached a new point in their relationship and formed a new closeness. He'd be content with that for now. It could have gone the other way. She could have turned her back completely. It wouldn't be the first time.

Innocent or not, the stigma of what he'd endured lingered in people's minds.

Back in the house, he stopped at the foot of the stairs, recalling the connection they'd made over their appreciation of the old house.

Their relationship had taken two steps forward this evening. He should be a happy man. But the shadow of Sara's eventual departure was always in the forefront of his mind. The store would open this weekend, and her obligation to her sister would be almost over. Once the babies came, Camille would no doubt take over, allowing Sara the opportunity to get back to the city. He might have grown closer to Sara, acknowledged their mutual attraction, but that didn't change the fact that his life was here in Blessing and hers was someplace else.

Sara placed the small cobalt blue vase with the single yellow rosebud on the café table the next morning, then scanned the area. With tables and chairs in place and the decorative elements positioned around the area, Sisters' Café was ready for business.

Sara smiled at the hand-painted sign beside the entrance to the eating area. It turned out her new hire, Alice Bailey, was a talented artist and had graciously designed the sign for the store. Sara had never considered a name for the café. She'd thought of it only as The New Again Café, but Camille had other ideas. When Sara protested, pointing out that the café had been Camille's idea, her sister had reminded her that without her help there would be no café or a store at all. She had sweetly added that she wanted to show her deep appreciation for all Sara's help and link them symbolically in the store's future.

Alice had also started a stencil for the plate glass window that would invite passersby to stop in for a quick drink or a snack. Coming to Blessing had seemed like being condemned to the wilderness, but now, seeing how the store had changed, spending time with her sister's family and even getting to know Luke had changed her way of thinking. The kindness of the locals was an added and unexpected gift.

Of course, she couldn't stay here once the store was back in Camille's hands. She had to earn a living, but in the future, she would be making more trips to visit. She'd come to think of Blessing as her home.

"Good morning, Sara."

Sara smiled as Alice came toward her. "Hello. I was just admiring your sign. It's perfect."

Alice nodded and patted her shoulder. "So you've told me. Repeatedly. I think you are more delighted by the name than the sign."

Sara couldn't argue. Alice was a good friend of Camille's. Having her working in the store was like having a family extension. Knowing Alice would be in charge gave Sara a great deal of reassurance.

"Your sister is over the moon that the café name will forever bond you together."

"It was very sweet of her."

"How's she doing? I'm tempted to call and

check on her, but I hate to wake her if she's sleeping."

"She's doing all right. There are good days and bad. Mostly she's ready for the babies to come. She doesn't like to be restrained."

Alice laughed. "Don't I know it. She's a real social butterfly. So, where do we start today? Tomorrow is the big day."

Sara throbbed with excitement. The grand reopening of The New Again Emporium. She'd wondered sometimes if the day would ever come. But thanks to Luke and Fred and her two new employees, they were ready to greet customers. "I have a bunch of errands to run, and we still have the door prizes to pick up, and I found a box of teacups and saucers in a box upstairs that we really should display."

"Oh, and the menu board for the café is ready for Luke to hang. Will he be here today?"

A very good question. She'd only spoken to him for a few moments since her discovery of his identity and the revelation of his past struggles. Things had felt different between them. There was a bond now, a new thread of understanding. But there was also a small sense of discomfort, as if neither of them knew where to go from here.

"I'm sure he'll be by at some point." What

she didn't know was how to approach him. There was a sense of walking on eggshells at times. She found herself measuring her words in an attempt to not say anything that would remind him of the secret she held or create concern that she might share it.

The irony of the situation played in her mind frequently. She'd spent most of her life hating secrets and surprises, yet here she was keeping Luke's secret and the aftermath of his surprising ordeal. Elliot had kept his to protect himself.

Now she was the one keeping a secret to protect Luke.

Luke entered the back door of New Again Friday afternoon and went in search of Sara. He'd been wavering between leaving her alone on this last day before opening so as not to interfere and wanting to be there just in case she needed him for any last-minute tasks. His desire to see her won. Stopping by the store wouldn't hurt anything, and it would make him feel he was helping in some way.

He found her back in a corner arranging cups on a decorative stand. "Are you going to work all night?" The smile she gave him made his pulse race.

"If I have to. I wondered if you'd come by today."

"I thought you might need some heavy lifting."

"Not yet. Just a few adjustments and lots of errands. Alice has been here while I run around town. She has been such a blessing. I know I'll be leaving the store in good hands when I go."

There it was. The shadow that hung over all his emotions. Sara would be leaving, and Jonah, too. He'd come to care for her son. He was a bright and inquisitive boy. He'd miss coaching him and teaching him basic woodworking skills.

"Did I hear someone mention my name?" Alice stepped around the cedar chest and handed Sara a small box with more cups. "This is the last of them."

As Sara arranged them on the shelves, Alice said, "I'm glad you're here, Luke. I wanted to ask you about the team celebration dinner. Marilyn and I have set it all up for next Friday night at seven at Mancini's Pizza. Is that all right with you?"

Sara tensed and glanced over her shoulder at him, reminding him of his rude response to her overtime request. He was committed to the weekly sessions. He hadn't missed one in three years. But the kids were looking forward to the dinner. Rusty and Jonah had been talking about it the other day at the workshop. He hated to see the disappointment in Sara's eyes, too. Maybe, just this once, he could get someone to step in for him.

"Friday is fine. I'll be there."

Sara's eyes widened, then warmed. He'd made the right decision.

Alice turned to go, then called over her shoulder. "Be sure you have a nice speech ready. The kids will want to hear praise from you."

Sara spoke softly, her eyes wary. "Are you sure Friday is good for you? I know you have a standing commitment."

"I'm sure. I don't want to miss the team dinner."

Sara's smile lit up the store. "Thank you." She laid her hand on his arm. "You won't regret it, Luke."

He already was, but he couldn't back out now. "I brought another chair for you. Not that you'll need it."

"Oh, really?" She set her hands on her hips. "I think it'll sell before we've been open an hour."

"Is that why it's covered up?" He'd noticed she'd draped a large sheet over the rocker. "Or are you afraid you'll scare people off when they see it?"

She chuckled and waved off his teasing. "No. That's to create excitement. I've had a lot of window peepers, and I want the chair to draw people in. I'm not going to uncover it until right before we open tomorrow."

"I think you're overly optimistic. It's just a chair."

"No, it's not. It's special."

"I can't take credit. My granddad designed it. All I did was follow his pattern."

She took his hand. "That's why it's special. His gift and your skill came together to make something rare and beautiful. An old traditional rocker made new again."

"The way you've made this store new again?"

"I hope so."

The way she was making him new again. He wanted her to know what she'd done for him, but her phone chimed, preventing him from speaking.

"Yes. That's fine. I'll be here. Come on over. Thank you."

Sara ended the call and looked at him.

Something in her expression made him concerned.

"That was a reporter from the *Blessing Banner*. He's on his way over to do an interview. He wants to print the article in the paper tomorrow."

Luke's throat tightened. "I'd better go." Old worries took on life again. The store was not even open, and he was getting attention. What would happen if Sara was right and the rockers took off? How would he handle it?

"Yes." She turned him toward the back door. "Go. I'll handle everything. Don't worry."

He nodded and made a quick exit. He was barely to his truck when his conscience flared. Maybe he should stick around and support Sara. But that meant running the risk of having to participate in the interview, having his picture taken, his face in the news.

Camille had been handling the social media end of things and had only referred to the chair as being created by a local artist. But that could all change after an article appeared in the newspaper.

Climbing into the safety of his truck, he cranked the engine and started for home. He probably should have stayed and helped Sara, but opening his life to a reporter was entirely different from sharing his past with Sara. It would be dangerous and foolhardy to risk being seen by the newsperson.

Luke's guilt and regret chipped away at his mood the rest of the day until he got inside his truck and headed back to the store. It was suppertime, but knowing Sara, she'd still be fussing over the store. The lights in the windows confirmed his suspicions and gave his heart a quick skip. It always did that when he was near her.

Inside the store he found her hunched over the checkout counter, studying her computer.

Thoughts of her had swirled in his head all afternoon, slowing his progress on his current project. He'd been forced to acknowledge that his whole attitude about his work had changed. He still derived a deep sense of satisfaction from his woodworking, but the feeling of escaping into it had disappeared. Now he was torn between maintaining his safe haven and stepping out into Sara's world.

The harsh reality was, other than mutual attraction, there was little else to keep them together. His feelings were strong, but there was still the matter of his strong need to protect himself. Besides, she was all set on moving away. He couldn't see a solution on either side.

The truth, however, couldn't keep him from needing to see her and be near her. It might be good for her to have a friend around tonight. The opening was only hours away. Right or wrong, he had to make sure she was prepared for the morning, and he had an idea what might just ease some of her stress.

He took a step toward her. "It's just me, Sara."

She looked up and smiled, her brown eyes curious. "What are you doing here so late?"

"I brought you a surprise."

She frowned, but there was a twinkle in her eyes. "You know it's dangerous to try and surprise me."

He stepped closer. "I'll risk it. You shouldn't be afraid of surprises. Some are very...sweet." He handed her a small box.

"What's this?" Slowly she opened the lid, then giggled. "A cinnamon roll."

Her eyes sparkled when she looked at him. "Perfect, because I'm starving. Let's share it." She took his hand and led him to one of the small tables in the café area.

"Won't you mess up your nice white tablecloths?"

"I'll fix it in the morning." She grabbed two forks from the service station and joined him.

"Hmm, this is delicious. You always know what will cheer me up."

"It's easy. As long as it's food." She swatted his hand. "I actually came by to see if you needed anything. I have an interest in this place, too."

"Yes, you do. I couldn't have done this without your help. And Fred's."

He took another bite of the sweet treat, gathering his courage to ask the question in the forefront of his mind. "How did the interview go?"

"Wonderful. I kept it all about me and Camille and the store."

Luke started to ask about his rocker, but she beat him to it. "I was intentionally vague about the rocker so you can sleep easy tonight. But Luke, I know these rockers are going to be a huge success. You need to decide what your role will be going forward. We can't keep it a secret forever."

Cinnamon roll consumed, Sara tossed the box in the trash. "I need to go. I'm all out of energy."

"I'll help you lock up." After turning off the lights and checking the locks, they stopped at the back door. Sara was chewing her lower lip, a sure sign she was nervous. He took her shoulders in his hands. "Stop. Everything is going to be fine tomorrow."

"I hope so."

"Have a little faith in yourself. I do. You're amazing."

She looked into his eyes, and his courage rose. He tilted her chin upward with one finger, lost in her brown eyes and dizzy with the heady scent of her perfume. There was no resisting now. No turning back. He had to know. He had to hold her close and know what her kiss was like. His senses spun as his lips touched hers. The world faded away, and only the two of them existed. When he ended the kiss, he was disoriented until he looked into her eyes and saw his own tangled emotions reflected there.

"Luke."

His name whispered softly on her lips sent his blood racing. "Sara."

No words were necessary. There was nothing to say. The kiss had changed everything, and he knew she was as befuddled as he was.

What it meant, however, he had no idea. What he wanted it to do was keep her at his side forever.

But was that a dream that could never be?

Chapter Nine

The excitement bubbling up from inside erupted in a small squeal of glee. Sara clasped her hands in front of her chin and grinned. The grand opening of The New Again Emporium and the Sisters' Café would begin in under an hour. She turned slowly, making one last inspection of the premises. The table and chairs were waiting to greet the first customers, and small bouquets of fresh flowers graced each place. Everything was perfect.

But just to be sure, she made a last-minute walkthrough of the vignettes, tweaking things here and there. Each grouping gave her a boost of energy. The store was so much more inviting now. Every display enticed customers around the next piece of furniture to see what was beyond.

Sara couldn't wait for Camille to see the results. She'd promised to send live videos during the day so her sister could share the fun.

"Sara. You in here?"

The sound of Luke's voice made her smile. She was glad he was here. He'd been such a big part of this project it was only right that he share in the day. She caught sight of him as she emerged from the grouping near the back of the store. Fred was with Luke. Her heart warmed. The family was all together.

They had become like family. Luke and Fred, Alice and the new part-time hire, Tricia Jones, had helped turn the store into a place you wanted to spend time in. Edith Pugh had managed the café with skill and a smile. "Good morning, gentlemen."

Luke smiled and held her gaze, causing a skip in her pulse. He looked good in dark jeans and a striped cotton shirt. An intriguing change from his usual carpenter pants and T-shirt.

"We thought you might need a few extra hands. Opening days can be hectic."

Fred nodded. "Right. We figured we could hang around to help out customers with loading their purchases or maybe make arrangements for deliveries." He held up his tablet.

"I've made a spreadsheet. I expect lots of orders."

Luke chuckled. "He's the optimistic one."

Fred winked. "Anything we can help you with before you throw open the doors?"

"No, all I have to do is uncover the rocker and unlock the doors. And try not to be sick." She pressed her hands to her stomach briefly.

Luke gave her a gentle look. "Hey. This is going to be a great day. You've worked hard, and the place looks incredible. You've transformed the store."

His support was touching and greatly appreciated. "I hope so. I want Camille to be pleased."

"Too bad she can't be here."

"I sent her a video tour this morning. She was really happy. That helps."

Sara checked the old grandfather clock near the checkout counter. Her hand went to her throat, and she bit her lip. "It's time." *Oh, Lord, please bless this day, for my sister's sake.* Luke's hand came to rest on her shoulder.

"You're not alone, Sara. Remember that."

She looked into his eyes, and her anxiety eased. He was such a thoughtful man. He always made her feel stronger, more capable.

"Thank you." She picked up the keys and took a deep breath. "Well, here we go."

She walked to the rocker and slowly pulled off the drape. A tingle of excitement chased through her being, and her spirits lifted. This rocker was meant to be in this store at this moment. She looked over at Luke. There were lines of tension around her mouth.

"Luke?"

"I'm, uh, going to be in the kitchen. This is your moment." He turned and strode toward the back. Fred sidled up to her.

"He's still a bit edgy over selling his work. It'll be okay."

She understood his reluctance better now. He had agreed to let people know his name, but he was still refusing to do any promotion beyond that. If her instincts were correct, the chairs would do all the promoting necessary. Word of mouth would carry the day.

Taking a deep breath, she slowly raised the old-fashioned blinds over the double glass door, turned the lock and pulled it open. A small crowd of shoppers waiting outside entered quickly. "Welcome to The New Again Emporium."

"Which is literally new again," a woman commented as she passed. Her companion breathed a soft sigh. "Look at this rocker. It's gorgeous."

Sara stepped toward the customer. "Let me tell you a little about this special piece."

The rest of the day was a blur. Customers milled around, many content to linger over every vignette. The hutch actually sold before the rocker, but Luke's chair didn't make it beyond the first half hour.

Alice spent most of the day at the register ringing up sales. Edith and her daughter, who had volunteered to waitress today, were kept on their toes. Luke and Fred made dozens of trips carrying purchases to trucks and cars, and Fred already had two full days of deliveries scheduled.

Sara was able to grab a small bite to eat in the kitchen before hurrying back to the sales floor. As promised, she'd sent Camille videos throughout the day, bringing happy smiles and even a moment of tears.

Closing had been announced twenty minutes ago, but a few stragglers weren't ready to leave. Finally, the last customer walked out the door, and Sara pulled down the blinds, set the lock and exhaled a slow, relieved sigh. Her body was drained of all energy yet exhilarated, at the same time.

Luke came through the store toward her. Had he read her mind? He was the first person she wanted to see. For a number of reasons. Not the least of which was she liked being around him.

"Well, did the day go the way you'd hoped?"

"Better. Ten times better. Camille is thrilled and I'm relieved. And vindicated."

Luke frowned. "Meaning?"

She gestured toward the empty space where the rocker once stood. "Both rockers sold. I'm going to need more. Can't have an empty space inside the front door."

Luke rubbed his chin and grinned. "You were right. I never would have guessed."

She raised her eyebrows. "Do you want to know what it sold for?"

His brows drew together. "I don't know. Do I?"

Sara grinned. "Would you believe it went for twice what I put on the tag? We actually started a small bidding war." She watched Luke's expression change to one of astonishment. It felt good to surprise someone. Maybe he was right. Not all surprises were bad.

"You can't be serious. Why would anyone pay that amount?"

"Because it's a work of art. A unique piece of craftsmanship. And it's from a local artist."

"You didn't tell them…"

"No, Luke, I didn't. But I told you it would sell quickly. And I told you that you could make a living off your carpentry. I have requests for five more chairs. Do you believe me now?"

"I may have to."

He ran his hand down the back of his neck, clearly bewildered by the value of his work. "I guess I'll be hauling a few more chairs over here."

She moved toward him and took his hand. "And maybe a table or two? I know you have a whole hayloft full of products in your barn."

Luke seemed to do a quick calculation in his head. "Hmm… I might have a future career in woodworking after all."

She remembered there had been inquiries earlier in the day about custom orders. "Luke…" She hesitated a little. "People have asked if you build on request."

His throat tightened. "What did you tell them?"

"The truth. I didn't know, but I'd check into it. You need to decide how you want to handle this. I'll work with whatever you decide. I think you should have business cards made, and I'll place them at the register. We can say that the rockers are your special craft, and you don't do anything else. However you feel comfortable."

This was what he must've dreaded. People wanting to know about him, about his work. She was on his side, and she'd work around whatever he decided.

He looked at Sara. "I have no idea what to do, because I didn't expect this outcome. I'll need to think about it."

"We'll work it out, Luke. In the meantime, let's enjoy the success your rocker has brought us both."

She slipped her arm around his waist. "I think I could use a double-decker sundae. Are you up for it?"

Luke laughed and started toward the back door. "I'll see that sundae and raise you one root beer float."

Sara leaned closer to his side as they walked, filled with more happiness than she'd known in a long time.

This would go down as one of the best days of her life.

Luke leaned against the doorframe of the kitchen, staring out into the sales area of the store as he drank his coffee. He had a clear view of the space Sara had chosen to display his work. He'd delivered two more rockers, a dining table and a bench. This was his third trip this week. Everything he'd brought had sold quickly, and his bank account was expanding. He should be pumped. He had a livelihood doing something he loved. His reputation as a craftsman was growing. Which meant his future was secured.

But for how long? He turned away and rinsed his cup in the sink. People were starting to recognize him even though he'd done his best to stay in the background. Sara was right. He couldn't produce good work and not expect to generate curiosity about its creator.

He'd tried to limit his time at the store, but maybe it was time to stay away completely. There was no logical reason to hang around. Sara had hired a few college students to help with the deliveries, and Fred had made himself available. The truth was, he liked being at the store. He liked being around Sara. He especially enjoyed sharing in her success. The New Again was a hive of activity. Sara had already had to open the café on a daily basis and take on extra help.

And his rockers were creating more and more interest. He'd already run out of business cards and had to order more. Most people would think that was a good thing. He was conflicted. He was getting too much attention, the one thing he'd wanted to avoid.

Pulling out his phone, he read the last message he'd received before coming here today. His blood chilled as he scanned it again. The assistant to State Senator Forrest Smith had requested information on the rocker. The senator was interested in purchasing one for his office.

Luke rubbed his lower lip. The situation was getting complicated. A new life was opening for him, but it could all go up in smoke if his past came out. Innocent or not.

"Luke, what are you doing back here? I thought you'd left."

He smiled as Sara came near. She seemed happy and glowing. The pink top and light blue jeans made her look as fresh as a spring flower. "The coffee smelled good. I couldn't resist."

"I'm so grateful for Alice. One sip of her coffee can make you feel so much better."

Something in her tone raised his concern. "What is it? What's happened?"

"Nothing."

She tilted her head at a defiant angle and shoved her hands into the pockets of her jeans.

Luke shook his head. "I know that expression. It's the one you wear when you've had bad news. Another rejection?"

Her shoulders sagged, and she nodded. "Yes. I had high hopes for this one. I'd decided to branch out and look at a few other jobs. Unfortunately, I'm either overqualified or underqualified. I don't seem to fit anywhere anymore."

"What do you mean?"

"Department stores are fading away, and the ones that remain are starting to rely on their managers to decorate the stores instead of hiring a full-time design staff. I thought about starting a business of my own, offering my services to smaller businesses, but so far that hasn't worked out, either. The cost of hiring me is out of line with their budgets."

"Surely one of the places you queried will come through."

"They'd better. There are only two left. One in Maine and one in California."

Luke's throat tightened. Both locations were as far from Mississippi as one could get. He would never see her or Jonah again. Except, of course, when they visited Camille. A dark cloud descended over his mood. The thought of never seeing Sara again, never hearing her sweet laugh, watching the emotions play across her face, was more terrifying than having his past exposed.

He was in too deep. With everything. He cared too much for her, and he'd risked his future by selling his work.

Sara straightened and squared her shoulders. He loved that about her. She never stayed down for long. "We need to get back to work. The festival starts at seven in the morning. It's the reason Camille wanted the store remodeled in time. And we made it." She bounced on her toes. "I can't believe it."

Luke set his feelings aside. All that mattered was making Sara happy. "I never had a doubt."

Sara peered out the front window of the store, smiling at all the activity. Blessing was bustling with visitors here to enjoy the day. The Blessing Bicentennial Arts and Crafts Festival was in full swing. Tented stalls were set up around the courthouse park on the square. The overflow was scattered along the main streets, which were being shared by food trucks and snack trailers. Shoppers were strolling through the various stalls looking for bargains and unique crafts. Alice had told her there were vendors from fifteen different states.

The Bicentennial committee had done a

wonderful job of promotion. Sara felt confident that some of those shoppers would wander into the New Again. To make sure, she'd placed a few enticing items on the sidewalk outside the front door to lure them in.

Sara made her way to the kitchen and headed for the coffeepot. She didn't usually drink three cups but today was a big day, and her nerves were a strange mix of anticipation, anxiety and satisfaction. She'd kept her promise to Camille and had The New Again Emporium open in time for the festival. And looking like a brand-new store. The kitchen had turned out beyond her expectation. It was gleaming and efficient. A far cry from the shabby space it was before.

All thanks to Luke.

The morning passed quickly with a steady stream of customers. All the rockers Luke had delivered were gone, each one selling as soon as she placed it on the floor. The café was always busy. Luke made a few deliveries and reported on the traffic jam on the roads. The festival was drawing huge crowds.

Sara finished refreshing a display in the far corner. The teacups had been a big hit. She was nearly out. She made a mental note to locate more. Making her way back to the checkout counter, she smiled when she saw Luke. He was talking to Alice. There was a conspiratorial expression on their faces. She frowned. "What?"

Alice smiled and winked at Luke. "You've been here all day. Why don't you take a break and check out the festival? I know you love all those arts and crafts things."

Sara liked the idea but the store was too busy for her to leave. She opened her mouth to protest but Luke cut her off before she could speak.

"Great idea, Alice. A change of scenery is just the ticket."

Sara looked between the two. Clearly they were in cahoots here. "I shouldn't. I need to change out the display on the—"

Luke shook his head and took her hand. "No time for plans. Just impulse. Besides, I'm hungry. The food truck up the block has chicken on a stick. Let's eat there."

Sara couldn't ignore her growing hunger or her longing to explore all the goodies on display. She looked at Luke. The glint in his eyes told her he would enjoy a day together, free from the concerns of the business and the responsibility of life.

"Go. Get out of here." Alice shooed them away. "I've got the store covered."

Luke grinned. "Live dangerously, Sara. Don't plan, don't think, just enjoy."

She gave in. How could she resist this man? "All right." They walked out the front door of the store and Luke steered them down the block. Chicken on a stick, a cool drink and a man to share lunch with were exactly what she needed.

She glanced up at him and squeezed his hand. "Thank you. I needed this."

"I know."

How did he know? Because he paid attention. He read her moods. He was sensitive to her situation. Those were things she'd never experienced before. It was an unfamiliar and exhilarating feeling. And she hoped it would continue.

Luke took the plate with the hot funnel cake and carried it to the bench at the edge of the courthouse park. Sara smiled and rubbed her hands together. "I love these things."

Luke chuckled and pulled off a piece for himself. Their time together this afternoon had passed too quickly for his liking. He'd ignored most of the monthly celebrations Blessing had held over the last year. Seeing the festival through Sara's eyes, however, was too big a temptation. She found delight and happiness in everything.

After eating lunch they'd wandered through the stalls, Sara taking her time in each one. She had a weakness for handmade jewelry. He made a mental note, just in case. He couldn't remember ever having such a wonderful time looking at arts and crafts. He'd even found a couple of woodworkers that had intrigued him. All in all, it had been a perfect couple of hours.

But Sara was getting anxious to check on things at the store.

She took one more bite, then stood. "Maybe we should nibble on this on our way back."

As they strolled down Main Street, Luke wished the day together would never end. Pulling off another piece from the powdered-sugar-covered funnel cake, she popped it into her mouth. The smile on her face gave Luke an idea of what she looked like as a child. He would never grow tired of being near her.

As they were almost at the New Again, Alice appeared out the front door and called to Sara. Sara waved, but Alice made a frantic motion for her to come quickly. Sara hurried ahead and disappeared inside the store.

When she emerged, her expression was one of fear and alarm. He froze. What had happened? He watched as she started down the sidewalk in the opposite direction. A man rose from a bench a short ways ahead and faced her.

Luke's senses went on alert. Sara stopped a few feet from the man, backing up quickly when he took a step toward her. Luke braced. Did she need help? Sara crossed her arms defensively across her chest, her shoulders stiff, her head held high.

Luke took a few steps closer. He couldn't hear what was being said, but their voices were growing louder. Sara shook her head, vigorously. The man held up his hands. She shook her head again, then waved him away and turned and hurried back toward the shop. The man watched her go, his gaze colliding with Luke's. A lance of protectiveness coursed through him. Whoever the man was, Luke would not let him hurt Sara.

The moment Sara saw him, she burst into tears and ducked into the shop. Luke hurried after her. Alice met him at the door. Her face reflected his own concern. "What is it? What happened?" she asked him.

"I don't know." He hurried to the back, finding Sara in the office. She was bent over, hands resting on the desktop and gulping in deep sobs. He went to her, pulled her into his arms and held her while she cried. Her fingers grasped the fabric of his shirt, clutching it like a lifeline. He made soothing sounds, holding her securely until the tears started to subside. "Sara, what happened? Can you tell me? Who was that man?"

She buried her face in his shoulder and muttered something.

"It's okay. I'm here. Just tell me what I can do."

"Nothing. There's nothing anyone can do."

She'd whispered the words so softly he wasn't sure he heard her correctly. "I saw you talking to him. That wasn't nothing. Please let me help you."

She stepped back, pulling a tissue from her pocket and dabbing at her eyes. She met his gaze, her dark eyes filled with sadness. "My ex-husband. Elliot."

Luke caught his breath. It was the last thing he'd expected to hear. His heart lurched. Did the guy want her back? "What was he here for?"

She sank onto the chair and scrubbed her fingers through her scalp. "He wanted to see Jonah."

"What did you tell him?"

"I told him no. Never. He lost that right when he abandoned us."

Luke waited for her to continue. He had a feeling this story would have to come in small segments.

Sara avoided his gaze when she continued. "We had a good marriage in the beginning. At least I thought so. But after Jonah was born he started spending more and more time away from home. He said he was working to make a better future for us, but he didn't spend much time with Jonah. He was always too busy. Then I found out he had another family."

"What do you mean?"

She bit her lip. "He had married someone else and they had two children. He'd been living two lives right under my nose. I never suspected a thing."

She fisted her hands on the desktop. "I was so stupid."

"Did that mean you were never married?"

"We were. I was the legal wife number one. He married the other woman in the third year of our marriage. Without bothering to get a divorce."

He took her hand and pulled up a chair beside her. "I'm so sorry."

"When his other wife found out, she turned

him in to the police. He was arrested and there was a big scandal. It was in the local papers. Nothing on the scale of what you endured, but humiliating nonetheless. I felt so embarrassed, so wounded and betrayed. It took nearly a year for the trial to start. Each time I thought I could put the whole thing behind me it would rise up and start all over again."

Now he understood how she could be so compassionate about his situation. "You didn't do anything wrong. He did this to himself."

Her lower lip puckered. "I was the poor clueless wife who had no idea her husband was cheating, let alone supporting another family. I obviously failed as a wife."

"Why is he looking for you now?"

"He finished serving his sentence for bigamy a few months ago and was looking for us. Apparently, his other family wanted nothing to do with him." The tears started again, and she clutched his arm. "What was wrong with us that he needed another family?"

He gently rubbed her back, wishing there was something he could say or do to soothe her pain. He knew from experience there were no words of comfort in this situation. "There was nothing wrong with you. The fault was in him. Any man would be proud and blessed

to have you as his wife and Jonah as his son."
He wanted to add himself to that statement
but held back. Now was not the time to share
his feelings.

She shook her head. "I've failed Jonah. I
robbed him of his father."

"No, you didn't."

She nodded dabbing at her eyes again. "Yes.
Don't you see? I have to make it up to him. I
have to give him the best life I can to make
amends."

"Sara, you've given him the only thing he
needs— your love."

She wiped her cheeks with her palms. "But
is love enough? Is it the answer?"

"Love is always the answer."

Luke believed it emphatically. He'd learned
the hard way that it was true, not only in romance but in every relationship. It was what
the Lord had told the world over and over and
in a million ways, but people still looked for
solutions and satisfaction elsewhere.

Would Sara come to believe it? And if she
did, would she see his true feelings in his eyes?
He hoped so, because it was becoming harder
and harder to mask his growing affection.

All he wanted now was to make her happy
and protect her from any more sadness. Now

he fully understood her aversion to secrets and surprises. She'd experienced two traumatic shocks in her life. Planning and staying in control was her way of coping.

He'd like to give her a life free of that. One where she could enjoy life's events and changes with anticipation instead of fear.

Would he ever get the chance?

Chapter Ten

Sara trailed her hand over the back of the Mc-Bride Rocker displayed in the front of the store Monday morning and smiled. Sales had exceeded even her high expectations. Luke had good-naturedly complained that he was running out of rockers, but she knew he was delighted with the outcome.

It was two days since Elliot had appeared at the store asking to see his son. The thought of his sudden arrival still sent a chill through her veins. She'd never imagined he would contact her. His behavior had said it all about his feelings toward his first family.

If it hadn't been for Luke's presence she would never have made it through. Her only thought had been to turn and run as fast as she could, which wouldn't have solved anything.

Luke had been her safe harbor in the storm. The one solid thing to hold on to.

"Thinking about Luke, aren't you?"

Sara blinked at the sound of Alice's voice. "What? No. Why would you say that?"

Alice fluttered her hands and batted her eyes. "You get all smiley and dreamy-looking. It doesn't take a genius."

Sara blushed. "I was, but not in the way you assume. I was thinking what a good friend he was the other day after Elliot showed up."

Alice nodded, a knowing smile on her face. "I noticed he was very solicitous. Do you think he'll be back? The ex, that is. He was very determined when he entered the store."

"I don't think so. I made it clear I didn't want to see him ever again. I have the law on my side in this matter." She could see Alice gearing up for a string of questions and quickly changed the subject. "It's almost time to open. We'd better get busy."

It was midafternoon when she heard Alice mutter a soft. "Oh no."

"What is it?" The expression on the woman's face raised Sara's concern.

Alice held up her cell phone. "Have you checked your social media lately?"

"No, why?" Sara's phone rang, and Camille's face appeared on the screen. She took the call, poked the speaker button and heard the hysteria in her sister's voice. "Are you all right, Camille? What's wrong?"

Camille had been in charge of the social media accounts since Sara took over, and while Sara kept tabs on it, she didn't check it every minute.

"It's on Twitter. You'd better look."

Alice held out her own phone, which was already displaying a tweet. Sara scanned it, the blood draining from her face in shock.

"Buyer beware. Those rockers you bought in the New Again Emporium were built by a killer. Do you really want to support a convicted criminal?"

"No. Oh no. Who did this? Why would they do this?"

"Check the name of the sender."

Sara knew the moment she read it who was behind the slander. Elliot. He must have recognized him when he was here. "No. No, he can't do this. Luke will be crushed."

"Do you know what this is about?" Camille asked.

"Yes. I'll tell you when I get home. Is there any way to stop Elliot from posting more about this?"

"I'll have Dave look into it. Is this true? Is Luke a convict?"

"It's complicated."

Sara hung up, her mind racing to find solutions for damage control. "This was Luke's worst nightmare."

Alice shrugged. "He's innocent. I looked him up. He didn't do it. He was wrongly accused. I knew it couldn't be true."

"But the damage it can cause is real." She spun at the sound of the back door opening. Luke. How could she tell him? Hurrying toward the kitchen, she intercepted him before he could enter the sales floor. "Luke, we need to talk." She took his arm and steered him toward the office. Where did she start? This was all her fault. She should never have pushed him to sell his chairs. There was no good way to broach the subject. "My ex has posted a comment about your past." He paled and set his jaw.

"What do you mean? What kind of comment?"

She handed him her phone. He leaned against the desk, then glanced upward. "I suppose it had to happen sooner or later. How did he find out?"

"I don't know."

"I think I might." Luke rubbed the bridge of his nose. "He stared at me a long time before he turned and walked away. He must have recognized me."

"He's doing this to get back at me because I refused to let him see Jonah."

Luke ran a hand down the back of his neck. "This is not good."

"Camille said it's only the one post, but how many people will see it?"

"It only takes one." He stood. "I'm going back to the farm. I need to think this through."

"Luke, I'm so sorry. I never dreamed he'd do something like this."

"It's not your fault. I should never have agreed to sell those rockers. I knew it was a risk, and now it's all coming out."

"Maybe it won't be that bad."

He laid his palm against her cheek. "I appreciate your optimism, but I don't think it's going to work this time."

Sara's throat tightened as she watched him leave. There was no way she could concentrate on work right now. She turned the store over to Alice and went home. She needed time to think and talk to Camille. For all her sister's fluff and fun attitude, she was very wise about a lot of life things.

Settled in Camille's bedroom a short while later, Sara clutched her cup of hot raspberry tea and tried not to cry.

"I had no idea about Luke's past. That's so awful. Though Dave told me he knew all along about his acquittal."

"How do you think the people of Blessing will react?" She gripped her cup like a lifeline.

Camille shrugged. "I think most will be understanding. Others not so much."

"I'm so worried about him. I feel responsible. I promised him I would keep his secret."

"And you did. He won't blame you."

"I just want to protect him."

"That's a natural reaction when someone we love is in danger."

Love? Did she love Luke? She'd pushed the thought aside, burying it deep in the back of her mind with all her other confused feelings. She'd had to repeatedly deny her emotional reaction to Luke when he was near. The kiss they'd shared the other night had kept her tossing and turning at night. She'd frequently wondered what it would be like to kiss him. She'd told herself once she did, she could set her emotions aside. Her curiosity would be satisfied. Only it hadn't worked out that way. Instead, she'd swayed like a swing in a windstorm between reliving the thrill of his kiss and trying to tell herself there was nothing serious behind it.

"Well, do you love him or not?"

Sara pulled her attention back to the current crisis. "I don't know."

One thing she did know: she was at the crossroads, and she'd have to decide soon. She couldn't keep her emotions tamped down much longer.

That kiss had unlocked a part of her that would never again be the same. Luke had changed her, given her a new point of view on life. One she fully intended to pursue.

But could she if he wasn't part of her plan?

Luke sought refuge in the cab of his truck. It was only two days since the tweet from Sara's ex-husband had appeared on social media, but the fallout had spread like a virus through Blessing. He'd come into town this morning to pick up a few things, but the stares and whispers had forced him to leave. It was like being yanked back in time. His throat tightened, and his blood chilled as a tsunami of painful memories surged through his mind.

He smacked his hand on the steering wheel. He'd been a fool to think he could live a normal life. He was innocent, but that didn't matter. The stigma was like a brand on his forehead. One he could never remove. Two boys had already been pulled from the team because of the rumors. Their parents had informed him that they would not be attending the team banquet this Friday as a result. He hated that the kids were being punished.

Fred met him at the barn as he got out of the truck.

"You weren't gone long. What happened?"

"What I expected. Stares, whispers from locals. Signs saying get out of town."

"Not literally, I hope."

"No, but it amounts to the same thing. The Carters and the McMillans have pulled their kids from the team and won't be at the celebration dinner."

Fred shook his head. "That's a shame."

Luke pulled his phone from his pocket, frowning at the number on the screen. "Hello."

"Is this Luke McBride?"

His stomach clenched. "Who's asking?"

"My name is Henry Bell. I'm with the *Blessing Banner*. I'd like to set up an interview. When would be a good time?"

"Never. I'm not interested."

"Wait. Don't you want to tell your side of the story? Get ahead of this thing?"

"There is no *thing*. I'm innocent. End of story."

"Yes, but…"

Luke ended the call. His mind swirled with memories, and his nerves burned with remembered humiliation.

"Luke, boy?" Fred touched his arm.

"That was a reporter wanting to tell my story." He shook his head. "It's starting all over again."

"No. It'll never be like that again. All that's in the past. You need to face this and end it."

"I intend to. I'm done."

"Son, you need to take a step back and clear your emotions. You have to talk to Sara."

"No."

Fred took his arm, forcing him to stop.

"Luke, she must feel awful about this. She'll blame herself. You know that. Besides, she's a friend. She'll help you sort this out."

Fred had a point. Sara had a way of clearing away the fog and giving him a new perspective on situations. She would be blaming herself, and he couldn't allow that. She'd kept her promise. He didn't want her feeling responsible for his situation.

Entering the store later that day, he started toward the front when he heard the voice of an agitated woman. He stopped, waiting for Alice and Sara to handle the situation. Sara's tone was calm and concerned when she spoke.

"Was there something wrong with the rocker?"

"Yes. A criminal made it. I won't have such a thing in my home."

"Mrs. Craddick, Mr. McBride is not a criminal. He…"

"Don't try and talk me out of this. I want to return the chair. I want my money back."

"Of course. Do you have your receipt?"

"Right here. You should have warned me about this man before I bought that thing. He shouldn't be allowed to even display his work in a decent place like this."

The pressure in Luke's chest made it hard to breathe. He'd never imagined something like this. His past was dragging down Sara's business, too.

"Would you like us to pick up the rocker, or will you be bringing it back?"

"I should say not. You can send one of your people to pick it up."

Sara's voice was tight, and Luke knew she was struggling to control her emotions. She ex-cused herself from the customer, and he heard Alice speak up.

"Miranda, you told me at church the other day how much you loved that rocker. You said it was the only chair you could sit in that didn't bother your back."

"That was before I knew who made it. I was shocked. Horrified."

"You do understand that Mr. McBride was acquitted of those charges. Someone else was responsible."

"It doesn't matter. He probably got off on a technicality. Rumors have basis in fact, you know."

"Yes, I do, and I know you do as well."

"What are you talking about?"

Sara rejoined the women at the counter.

Alice peered over her glasses. "As I recall, your boy Wesley was accused of assaulting a young woman last year. He was even arrested."

"That was a lie. He never touched her. She made the whole thing up."

"True. Wesley was innocent, but that didn't stop people from thinking the worst. So much so that he left for college early to escape the situation."

"Can you blame him? People were brutal."

"So you do understand about being wrongly

accused. The suspicions linger even if they aren't warranted. Like in Luke's situation."

"That's different."

Sara noticed the woman's tone had lost much of its anger.

"Is it?" Alice handed the woman a receipt. "I've credited your account."

There was a long silence. Luke held his breath.

"Well, maybe I've been a bit hasty. Perhaps I'll keep the chair after all. I'll think it over a little more."

Luke heard footsteps, then the bell over the entrance jingle as the customer left.

Sara touched Alice's arm. "What did you say to her?"

"I reminded her of a time in her own life when the truth was overlooked and innocence ignored. Miranda isn't a bad person, but she tends to judge others without knowing all the facts first. I doubt she even looked beyond that rumor about Luke."

Luke spun on his heel and left the store, a growing conviction forming in his chest. He had to put an end to this mess. Fast. It was bad enough that the town was ready to tar and feather him, but he couldn't allow his shadow to fall on Sara. He realized now that no matter where he went, no matter how innocent he was, his past would always intrude. The stigma would always be there. He couldn't put that burden on Sara. She was already dealing with a husband who was a bigamist. She didn't need a friend who was an assumed murderer.

He stopped his truck in front of his workshop, pulled out his phone and made the call. His life in Blessing was at an end. He'd have to start over someplace else.

Friday morning, Fred stormed into the workshop, a deep scowl marring his craggy features. "What do you think you're doing?"

Luke didn't have to ask what he meant. The For Sale sign had gone up at the end of the drive first thing this morning. "Selling out."

"Running out is more like it. What brought this on?"

Luke told him about the customer at the shop.

Fred growled in his throat. "I know Miranda Craddick, and she loves to create drama. Anything that calls attention to herself. Alice was right to put her in her place. She's quick to judge others and slow to look at her own dirty linen."

Luke set his jaw. "You're missing the point.

As long as I'm here, people will link Sara with me, and she'll suffer for it. The best thing for everyone is to walk away. I can't let her be burdened by something she had no part in."

"That sounds all noble and good, but Luke, you're going about this all wrong. It's time you turned and faced the world and said, *No, I'm not guilty, and you can't make me feel that way anymore.*"

The truth in his friend's statement washed through him like a cold spray. He had a point. This didn't involve only him. He could withstand the harsh judgment while the town adjusted. He knew they'd eventually find something else to fuel their rumor mill, but in the meantime Sara's business could suffer and she'd be guilty by association. And what about Jonah? How would it affect him?

Luke shook his head, keeping his back to Fred.

"Right. Well, I can see you're not listening to anything I have to say." He turned and walked to the door. "I hope you're still going to the celebration dinner for the team tonight. Those kids are counting on you."

Fred left without waiting for a reply, which Luke knew meant his question was more of an order than mere curiosity. Attending the dinner was the last thing he felt like doing, but he enjoyed coaching the kids, and he'd promised Sara he'd attend. She'd kept her promise, so the least he could do was keep his.

He was dressed and ready to walk out the door to start for the restaurant when the phone call came. His heart sank to the pit of his stomach. He'd been asked to stop by his meeting. His presence was needed urgently. He checked his watch. If he hurried, he could stop by the meeting, handle the situation and still make it to the dinner. He'd be a little late, but he'd be there. He offered up a prayer. First, that he'd be able to defuse the issue at his meeting, and second, that Sara would understand his tardiness.

Why was his life suddenly becoming so complicated?

Sara craned her neck to look at the entrance of the party room at the restaurant where the team dinner was being held. The celebration had started a half hour ago, but Luke had yet to arrive.

Marilyn nudged her shoulder. "He'll be here. I'm sure."

Sara set her jaw and tried to tamp down her rising irritation. "He'd better. These kids will be so disappointed." Not to mention how furious she would be. She'd tried to contact him, but he'd not answered either her calls or her texts. He was usually quick to respond. Her first thought was that he'd backed out and had chosen to attend his secret Friday meeting instead. She didn't want to believe that.

She took a sip of her cola and glanced around the party room. Everyone was getting anxious. She had nothing to tell them. Harold Young approached her table. He had served as assistant coach this season.

"Any word from Luke?"

"No. But I'll keep trying."

"Should I start the proceedings? He can always take over when he gets here, but the kids are getting restless."

She wanted to decline. She wanted to believe that Luke would not let her and the team down, but they couldn't wait any longer. "Go ahead. Thank you."

Harold smiled. "I'm sure he has a good reason for being late."

She nodded. Did he? Or had he taken to hiding out again? The rumors about him were slowly fading, but there had been a few very vocal residents who refused to listen to reason.

Marilyn met her gaze. "Maybe facing everyone was just too difficult right now."

Sara worked her jaw. "It's possible, but hasn't he played hermit long enough? There comes a time when the hiding has to stop."

She couldn't believe Luke would suddenly revert. They'd taken a new step forward in their relationship. Sharing their secrets had drawn them closer and given them a bond of understanding. At least that was what she'd assumed when he'd put this dinner above his Friday commitment. It was the one secret he still kept from her. She'd assumed that his agreeing to come to the dinner meant he was ready to open up to her completely. But now her old nagging fear of secrets and surprises was coming to life again. Still, she'd vowed to withhold her judgment until they had a chance to talk.

By the time the last family left the restaurant, Sara's belief in Luke had evaporated. Despite Luke's absence and a few snide remarks from certain parents, the celebration had been a success. Harold had proved to be an entertaining master of ceremonies and had something fun to say about each player. Even Jonah and Rusty had overcome their disappointment.

She, however, had not. Her chest was tight as she gathered up the last of her belongings and headed for the door. It was one thing to break a promise to her. She was an adult, and she could survive. Letting down the players, however, was another matter altogether. There could be no excuse for that.

Luke struggled to swallow around the tightness in his throat. This was never supposed to happen. Security at the area prison was top-notch. Yet here he was, caught up in a hostage situation.

He'd come to the prison to comfort one of his Bible study members who was struggling emotionally. They'd been talking through his issues and making progress. Unfortunately, the weekly study group had turned into a dangerous standoff with an inmate who had forced himself into the study room brandishing a gun. He was threatening to shoot anyone who crossed him and making outrageous demands. Luke, along with nine Bible study inmates, a guard and the church member Luke had enlisted to take his place tonight, were all trapped until the authorities could sort out the mess.

Luke was seated next to Ron Knudson, one of the deacons at his church. "Sorry I talked you into this."

Ron spoke softly. "You didn't know this was coming. Besides, we both realize we're here for a reason, right?"

Normally, Luke would have agreed. He was always on the lookout for a chance to share the good news. But tonight, he had other matters of concern. Mainly regret that he hadn't told Sara the nature of his Friday night commitment. It seemed silly now, but at the time, he didn't want to share something so important to him with a woman he barely knew. Now she would be angry that he wasn't at the dinner, because she had no idea what he did. Yet another surprise that would reinforce her conviction that surprises were always bad.

Ron whispered. "Maybe we can talk to this guy. Appeal to his better nature."

Luke swallowed the bitter laugh that rose in his throat. He'd learned the hard way that few prisoners had a better nature. There were those who did, and those were the ones that normally signed up for Bible study. "I think this guy is more interested in breaking out than his salvation."

Luke checked his watch. The dinner had started half an hour ago. Sara would be looking for him. His chest burned. She would never forgive him, let alone trust him. Jonah and Rusty would hate him. His standing with the parents would be destroyed, and the rumor mill would ramp up again.

He hoped one of the dads who helped as assistant coaches would take over the awards portion. He hated that he wouldn't get to hand Jonah and Rusty their trophies. He was so proud of all the players.

"How long before the cops get here to handle this mess?"

Luke saw the fear in Ron's eyes. "No idea. I suggest you start praying."

"I started the moment I walked in here."

Luke echoed the statement with a nod. Their situation was in the Lord's hands now.

He believed the Lord would deliver them. He just didn't know how or when, and that was the hard part.

"Come on, boys. Let's get home." Sara gathered up her belongings and headed for the parking lot.

Every nerve in her body was vibrating with anger. Her heart thudded against her rib cage, beating out one word. *Stupid*. Once again she'd allowed herself to fall for the wrong man, and opened her heart when she should have been protecting it.

Luke had missed the banquet. He hadn't sent a text, phoned or relayed a message. He simply hadn't shown up. The disappointment was evident on the players' faces. Thanks to Harold, the evening had still been fun for everyone.

Except her.

Her mind ran through several scenarios of how she would deal with the man when she saw him. Maybe she'd scream her lungs out. Maybe she'd kick him in the shins, or maybe she'd give him such a cold shoulder he'd see snow in south Mississippi.

Jonah held up his gold trophy. "I'm going to find a special place for this in my room."

"No." Rusty shook his head. "Let's put them on the mantel where everyone can see them."

Sara let their chatter swirl around as they thought of more and more outrageous places to display their new awards.

She walked across the parking lot toward the car, watching as Rusty and Jonah slid into the back seat. Suddenly very tired, she looked forward to getting home and hiding in her room. Her phone rang as she reached for the handle. Dave's name popped up, sending a lance of alarm along her veins. "Dave? Is everything all right?"

"Camille has gone into labor. We're at the hospital in Hattiesburg. I need you to bring Rusty here. Camille wants him nearby."

The tone of Dave's voice suggested he wasn't

telling her everything. "Okay. We're just leaving the banquet. I'll come straight there. How is Camille?" Dave's silence knotted her stomach.

"We'll talk when you get here."

"Buckle up, guys. We're going to the hospital. Rusty, your mom is going to have those babies."

"Cool. I want to see them."

Sara struggled to breathe against the tightness in her chest. She didn't want to cause Rusty any worry, but she wasn't sure she could contain her own fears. She reached the hospital in record time and joined Dave in the waiting area of the maternity floor. The sight of him sent a chill through her body. He looked terrified. He immediately went to his son and took him aside. Sara's throat constricted. Dave's posture as he spoke to Rusty suggested he was delivering bad news.

Finally, Dave approached her, his expression lined with worry. It was all she could do to wait for him to speak.

"Camille is fine at the moment, but the doctor is concerned about her blood pressure, along with her other issues. I don't know any more than that right now. I'm going to take Rusty to see his mom, but I'll keep you informed."

Sara pulled Jonah to her side. "We'll be here if you need anything. Give her my love."

"Mom, is Aunt Camille going to be okay?"

"We hope so." She guided him toward a small sofa in the corner near the window. "She has the best doctors taking care of her."

Jonah rested his head against her shoulder. "Is having babies dangerous?"

Sara squeezed him gently. "Not usually, no."

A short while later Rusty came out and joined them, his head lowered. "Was she glad to see you?"

Rusty nodded. "But she hurts. They took her to a different room, and Dad made me come out here. I wanted to stay with her."

"I know, but the doctors need room to work. It's best if you stay out here with us." She didn't like what she'd heard. Camille had suffered from various issues during this pregnancy. Sara had still prayed that delivery would be quick and simple.

She did her best to comfort Rusty, but he was silent and withdrawn. Jonah had a thousand questions. Sara explained the situation to her son as simply as possible and hugged him. She wished there was someone to hug her. She was still angry at Luke, but right now, she longed for nothing more than his strong arms of support.

"Mom, can't we help Aunt Camille somehow?"

"Pray. Pray hard." She rested her head on his.

"What do I say?"

"You don't have to say anything. The Lord understands your heart."

For her part she lifted up every portion of her heart and asked for safety for her sister and the little ones coming into the world.

Nothing else mattered. Not a job, or the store or Luke. Everything took second place to the well-being of Camille.

Chapter Eleven

Dave joined them a short while later. The lines in his face had deepened, raising Sara's concern. He pulled her aside, lowering his voice. "It's not looking good. The doctors aren't sure they can save both babies. They're worried about Camille, too."

Sara wrapped her arms around her brother-in-law. "She's strong and she's bullheaded. You'll see. She'll fight through this."

He nodded; tears appeared in his eyes. "I've got to get back to her. You don't have to stay."

Sara shook her head. "I'm not leaving until I know everything is all right. I'm sure the boys will want to be here, too."

It was nearly an hour later when Sara heard someone call her name. She looked up to find Fred staring down at her. "What are you doing here? How did you know I was here?" He sat down beside her, closer than she expected, sending alarms through her mind.

"Pastor Miller told me where to find you."

The more she looked at Fred the more her alarm grew. "Are you here about Camille?"

"No. I'm here about Luke."

Blood drained from her face. She grabbed Fred's arm. "What is it? What's happened?"

Fred held her hand. "Have you seen the news?"

"No. Why? Fred?"

"There's a situation at the prison, and Luke has been caught up in it."

He wasn't making any sense. "Why was Luke at the prison?"

"He leads a Bible study there every Friday night."

Sara was beginning to think she was dreaming. Nothing was making sense. "He was supposed to be at the dinner."

"I know. He found someone to take his place, but then he got a call to stop by. When he did, he got caught up in a…situation."

Sara pressed her fingers against her temples. Still struggling to comprehend. "Are you saying he's been taken hostage?"

Fred nodded. "Along with several others.

The authorities are trying to defuse the situation, but they're at a standstill."

She started to ask more questions, then realized she wouldn't like any of the answers. "Luke. Oh, Lord, please don't let anything happen to him." Tears filled her eyes. Fred wrapped an arm around her shoulders.

"I know this is the worst news to give you under the circumstances, but I thought you should know."

She nodded. Her body pulsated with waves of heat and cold and a loud ringing in her ears. "Why didn't he tell me? Why was it such a big secret?"

Fred met her gaze. "Luke is a very private man. The trial exposed him and scarred him deeply. He didn't want attention of any kind ever again."

Sara nodded. She'd realized that about him and she understood, but they'd become close. He could have confided in her. She rubbed her forehead. None of that mattered now. He was in danger.

Dave suddenly appeared in front of them looking worn and haggard. She forced her thoughts back to her sister.

He nodded to Fred. "I don't have anything to report. Things are touch and go. We'll just have to wait. I've called my parents. They'll be driving up from the coast to watch Rusty."

Fred stood. "Why don't I take the boys home and stay with them until your folks show up?"

"That would be a big help. Thanks. Sara, you can go, too."

"No. I'm staying." The last thing she wanted now was to be alone. But she didn't really want to be here, either. Her heart was so heavy with worry it lay like a stone in the center of her chest. Her mind churned between worry over Camille and the babies and Luke.

She glanced round the waiting room after Fred and Dave left. It was empty for the moment. She changed the TV channel to watch the news. The anchor was giving the latest report on the hostage situation. A video was playing in the background of law enforcement surrounding the prison. Bile rose in her throat. Her whole being rejected the idea of losing Luke.

Sara stood searching for direction. She couldn't stay here, but she couldn't leave, either. There must be someplace quiet she could go, to think. And pray. After inquiring about the hospital chapel, she made her way down the hall and slipped inside the small room. Taking a seat in the second row, she let her gaze rest on the simplicity of the altar. A single cross, an open Bible and a candle.

Her anxiety eased as she sought words to pray. None came. Only tears that soon became sobs. She cried out to God, though she didn't form any coherent thought. She recalled what she'd told her son. Thankfully, the Lord knew what we wanted to say even if we didn't.

Wiping her eyes, she inhaled a deep breath. It was easier to breathe now, though her heart was still heavy. What would she do if she lost her sister or one of the babies? Camille would be devastated. And Luke… She'd only just admitted she loved him, and now he was caught up in a situation that could cost him his life.

Slowly, her thoughts began to coalesce on Luke. Now she knew his last secret. The Friday night commitment he refused to change. She never would have suspected he was leading a Bible study with the inmates of the prison. Tender warmth spread through her veins. She should have guessed. Luke made no secret of his faith even though he rarely mentioned it aloud. It was evident in his actions and behavior and his presence at the church every Sunday.

Her own faith could use a booster shot. Especially now. She bowed her head again and asked the Lord to increase her belief.

Somewhat fortified, Sara returned to the waiting area, her gaze drawn to the TV screen again. The situation was still volatile. Police negotiators had been called in, and a spokesman from inside was relaying information back and forth. Her palms began to sweat. She'd never felt so alone or so trapped and helpless. There was nothing she could do for her sister or Luke but pray, and while she knew that was vital, she wished she could do something tangible.

The news ended, and she turned off the TV. She couldn't bear any more bad news. Taking a seat up in the corner of the room, she stared out at the night sky. The situation had uncovered one important fact. She loved Luke. A truth she'd been ignoring for weeks. She'd been ignoring a great many things she'd learned about him, because she'd been filtering them through her own failures and not trusting her emotions.

"Sara."

Dave came toward her, his smile lighting up the room. "They're here and they're perfect. A little boy and a little girl. They're small but otherwise healthy."

Sara rushed to him. "Thank God. What happened? I thought things weren't going well."

Dave shrugged and ran a hand through his

hair. "I don't know. One minute things looked bad, then suddenly it all came together. I guess the Lord wanted those babies to join our family."

"Camille?"

"She's fine. Exhausted but happy. I have to get back. Will you be okay?"

"Of course." She motioned him away. "Go."

Sara buried her face in her hands, lifting prayers of gratitude with a thankful heart. Now she could focus on the other important person in her life. Luke. Grabbing the remote she turned on the TV again. The picture this time had a different story. The hostage situation was over. The negotiators had talked the man down. The screen showed images of Luke and another man being escorted out of the prison and into police cars, then driven off. Her knees buckled. He was safe. He was alive. She had to see him for herself. To touch him and know he was all right.

She had to tell him she loved him.

Her hand went to her throat. He must be hurting. It was happening again—the spotlight, the stares, the accusations. She had to help him. She could be his buffer. He needed her now. Her hand shook as she pulled out her phone. She willed herself to calm down.

It was nearly midnight when Sara neared

home. Bypassing her sister's driveway, she went straight to Luke's and pulled up to the house. It was dark. She tried texting him again. She'd sent a dozen messages since leaving the hospital and at least five emails and six phone calls. He hadn't answered any of them. Where could he be? She'd seen him walk out of the prison. Had he been taken to the hospital? Had he been hurt? Her mind was swirling with ugly possibilities. She had to see him. She fought back panic. "Where are you?" A quick call to Fred didn't provide many answers, either.

"I haven't heard from him. But when I do I'll let you know first thing."

Luke slipped behind the wheel of his truck, still parked in the prison visitors' lot, and took a deep breath. It had been a long, frightening evening, but he was free and safe. He should be grateful for those two things, but the knot in his gut didn't ease up. All's well that ends well, but he couldn't shake the aftermath of the night's events so easily. Once again, he'd found himself in the middle of a media barrage. Reporters and cameras were waiting as he and Ron were escorted out of the prison. They'd hovered like vultures at the police station while he and Ron had been questioned and debriefed for what seemed like hours. The old sense of being exposed had returned full force, and all he wanted to do was go home and hunker down.

Actually, there was one other thing he wanted to do: see Sara. Her soothing presence would ease all his tension. But he had no idea how she felt about him right now. He knew she would be furious and crushed that he'd missed the team dinner. Had she heard about the situation at the prison? Would she realize he was involved? He'd never confided his reason for being busy on Friday night. What would she think?

He pulled into his drive, catching sight of the For Sale sign. Now more than ever he was sure he'd made the right decision to leave Blessing. As much as he loved Sara, tonight's events reinforced his belief that he was not the right man for her. His past would forever cast a pall over their lives. They'd always be on edge, never knowing when it would be uncovered, and the attention would rob them of their privacy.

As he neared the house, he saw his parking area filled with cars and a local network TV truck. The vultures were waiting to pick his bones. Pulling sharply into the grass, he turned around and drove away. He couldn't even go home to lick his wounds.

Yes, leaving town was the only reasonable solution. He'd started over once, and he could do it again. This time he'd do things differently. He'd find a new way to a earn living. There were always jobs for rough-in carpenters. He'd simply stay away from designing fancy rocking chairs. Leaving Sara and Jonah behind, however, was not going to be as easy.

He checked into a hotel in the next town, but sleep and peace eluded him, no matter how much he prayed or berated himself for his weakness. At daylight he headed home, guessing that the reporters wouldn't still be lurking at that early hour. Thankfully, his hunch was good, and his driveway was devoid of any strange vehicles. Safely inside his old house, he pulled out his phone and called Fred, ignoring the numerous calls, texts and emails from an obviously worried Sara. He couldn't postpone that encounter much longer. But he wasn't looking forward to facing her.

After reassuring his friend he was all right and giving him a brief rundown of last night's events, Luke made a pot of coffee and tried to regroup. He spooned sugar into his cup, but the sound of a car approaching caused him to freeze. Were the reporters back on the job so early? Maybe if he didn't move, they wouldn't sense his presence.

"Luke."

Someone was pounding on his front door.

"Luke, open up, please. I have to see you."

Sara? How had she known he was home? Fred. He should have known he would call her.

He hurried to the door and opened it, the sight of her soothing his heart with the only warmth he'd known in twenty-four hours. She stared at him, her eyes misting over.

"You're all right?" She stepped forward, hands coming to rest against his chest as if he were fragile.

He took her hands in his. "I'm fine. No worse for the wear."

Tears trickled down her cheeks, and she wrapped her arms around his chest holding him tight.

"I was so scared. I was afraid I'd lose you."

Luke pulled her close, filled with a sense of permanence and belonging. "So was I. I wanted to get back to you and Jonah. I'm sorry I missed the dinner."

Sara shook her head. "It's okay. I understand, but why didn't you tell me what you did on Fridays? I would have understood. Fred explained it to me. And why didn't you take my calls? I could have helped you." She took a step closer. "They're saying you were a hero and ended the standoff."

Luke shook his head. "No. Ron and I just tried to keep everyone calm. The inmate came around on his own."

He gently squeezed her shoulders. "I'm sorry I didn't answer you. The reporters were waiting. I couldn't deal with that, and I needed time to decompress."

"Alone?"

He nodded, painfully aware of how selfish he sounded. He didn't like seeing the disappointment in her pretty eyes. He searched for a different topic. "How's Camille? Fred told me about the complications."

"They're all fine. She and the babies will stay in the hospital for a time, but they should be home soon."

"I'm sorry I wasn't there to help you."

Sara stepped back, searching his face with her gaze. "I saw the For Sale sign at the road. What are you doing, Luke?"

There it was: the conversation he'd dreaded. "It's time to move on, that's all."

"Why? What's changed?"

"Everything. Don't you see? First the town

finds out about the trial, then the hostage situation pushes me into the spotlight again. Nothing will ever change. I'll always be looking over my shoulder, waiting for the next camera to pop out of the bushes and strip me bare."

"Don't you think you've lived that lie long enough?"

Her question shocked him. She was usually so sympathetic and compassionate. "What?"

"This excuse you cling to that your past has labeled you forever and somehow disqualifies you from having a life."

"It's not an excuse."

"Isn't it? The town didn't turn its back on you when your past was revealed. Only a few people took notice. No great flood of reporters showed up. Don't you think it's time you let go of that crutch? Stop seeing yourself as guilty. Stop trying to shield yourself from any kind of attention and just live your life. Stop hiding behind the fear."

Luke set his jaw. What right did she have to cast judgment on him? "And what about you, Sara? Aren't you hiding?"

"No."

"Oh? What do you call your incessant planning? Always trying to see around corners, make sure you have everything covered so you can deal with any surprises that might crop up. If that isn't fear, I don't know what is."

She pressed her lips together. "I have a son to consider. I have to plan ahead. I can't just up and change directions on a whim."

Luke ran a hand through his hair. "Sara, I'm only thinking of you. I don't want to burden you with this albatross I live with. It wouldn't be fair. Your life would always be on edge. I care for you too much to do that."

"Me? You're thinking of me?" She shook her head, her eyes darkening.

Luke braced, realizing he'd poked a hornet's nest. He'd never seen Sara this angry. She was vibrating with emotion.

"That's the same excuse my dad used when he put off telling us he'd lost his job. He didn't want to upset us. Elliot had the same poor reason for his behavior. He didn't want to ask for a divorce because it would be too upsetting for me. You're no different. All of you were selfish, doing what's best and easiest for yourselves."

Tears streamed down her cheeks. He knew reaching out to her now was a mistake. "Sara."

"I thought you were different. I thought you were a man I could… I thought we had something special."

"We do. I love you, but because I do, I won't risk exposing you to the shame and harassment that would bombard us if the past was uncovered."

Sara shook her head and held up her hands in defeat. She turned and marched out, slamming the door behind her and leaving him with a sick knot in his chest that threatened to choke him.

He'd lost her, and the worst thing was, he knew she was right. She'd pegged him perfectly. He'd used the workshop and this house as a fortress, a way to protect himself from being hurt and exposed again. He'd convinced himself he was here healing, restoring his emotional equilibrium. Slowly, he walked down the hall to the kitchen, realizing with a jolt that he'd harbored the hope that Sara would help him fix it up one day. Somewhere along the way, Sara had become part of all his future plans. But he'd shut that dream down as easily as he shut off his table saw.

He needed to get her back, but he had no idea where to start. He sank onto the stairs, forearms on his knees, as he struggled to conquer his emotions. He saw no simple solution.

He wanted Sara in his life, but he'd chased her away. The peace and safety he'd once found in his workshop no longer held the same comfort and appeal.

If only he could make things right between them. He knew he couldn't accomplish that on his own. He'd messed up too badly, and he had no idea where to start. Or maybe he did. What he needed was more than his own understanding.

The rest of the day passed in a haze. Thankfully, there was enough work at the store to keep Sara's mind occupied, but the heartache refused to ease. It wavered between being angry that she'd messed up again and pain at losing Luke. She loved him, but it would never work out, not as long as he kept hiding behind an old event, one that should have been overcome a long time ago.

She thought they'd understood one another, but she'd been wrong about that, too. He'd accused her of hiding. So not true. She hadn't hidden from anything. She'd walked into Blessing eyes wide open, tackled the job at hand and turned it around. His lack of understanding was just another sign that they weren't right for one another.

So why wouldn't her heart let go?

One of the antique clocks struck five, and

Sara exhaled in relief. Finally, this day was at an end. She could go home. Her phone rang just as she turned the lock on the front doors. The name on the screen sent her hopes into orbit. Lazarus Department Stores. It was the last big chain in the country and the last application she'd submitted. When she hung up the phone a few minutes later, her spirits were soaring. The job offer was better than she'd ever imagined. The only drawback was that it was in San Francisco. Farther away from Blessing than she'd hoped. She'd grown fond of the small town and being close to her family. Still. It was clearly an answer to her prayers. The Lord had opened a door, a clear path to her future, and it was right in line with her plan.

The offer was only good for a short while. They needed an answer quickly. She would stop by the hospital on her way home and tell Camille the good news. And check on her new niece and nephew, of course.

She locked the back door and strolled to her car, wondering when the sense of elation would arrive. The initial thrill of receiving the offer had faded quickly, and she'd been left feeling an unexpected letdown. Probably just a reaction to finally getting a job. She'd been on an emotional roller coaster for a long time. The joy would come later.

Sara drove toward the hospital, eager to talk to her sister. For all their differences, Camille always had a way of helping Sara see things from another perspective. She needed that now. Her heart wanted to discuss the new job with Luke, but that was out of the question now. They weren't even on the same page any longer.

Tears stung her eyes. How had things turned sour so quickly?

By the time she reached her sister's room, Sara had decided to keep her conversation focused on her new job and not mention Luke at all. She didn't trust her emotions right now, and Camille didn't need anything to upset her.

"They are beautiful. So tiny." Sara sat on the edge of the bed beside her sister. "When can you come home?"

"Soon. The doctor wants to keep them under observation for a while, but he's very encouraged. They're strong and healthy."

"Have you chosen names yet?"

"Yes. Robert and Rebecca."

Sara smiled. "Perfect. All *R*'s to go along with Rusty, uh, Richard."

Camille narrowed her eyes and frowned.

"Okay, what's going on? Something has happened."

"Yes. I had a job offer today. An incredibly good, unbelievable offer."

"That's wonderful. I know how discouraged you've been. Tell me all about it."

"Great pay, plus I'd be in charge of the entire visual department and even have a say in the overall design of the entire chain." She paused and took a fortifying breath. "But it's in San Francisco."

Camille's smile faded. "Oh, that's so far away. I was hoping you'd be closer. I've gotten used to you being here. I wanted to have some time together when I'm back to normal and not tethered to a bed all day."

"I know." Sara squeezed her hand. "I was looking forward to that, too, but you'll be back on your feet soon and able to take over the store. Alice can run things until you're on your feet. I know you've been looking forward to it for a long time."

Camille nodded without speaking. "I wanted to know about Luke also. Have you talked to him? That was a scary thing he was involved in. Dave and I found out about it later. You must have been a wreck."

"I was. It was a long night. But it all turned

out all right. You and the twins are fine, and Luke is safe. I spoke with him briefly." Sensing a barrage of questions, Sara stood and kissed her sister goodbye. "I hate to run, but it's been a long twenty-four hours. I'll stop by again tomorrow. Anything I can do at home to get ready for your homecoming?"

"No. Dave's folks have it all under control."

Sara berated herself on the drive home for skirting the issue of Luke with her sister. She wasn't ready to share her feelings yet. Her emotions were still too raw. First, she had to tell Jonah about the move. She wasn't looking forward to it. Her son loved living in Blessing. He'd be upset, but he'd come around. They'd visit often, and she'd promise to send him back to Blessing for summer vacation and all the holidays. He was old enough to understand the situation. The sooner they started this journey the better. The time had come to put the past behind her and move on.

Sara arrived at the house as Rusty and his grandparents were leaving for the hospital to visit Camille. She welcomed their absence. It would give her plenty of time to talk to Jonah. She found him in the bonus room upstairs, playing a video game. She watched him for a moment, her heart filling with pride. She loved him so much. She had so many plans for his future. Her new job would mean she could fulfill all her dreams for him.

She touched the top of his head. "Hey, kiddo. We need to have a talk."

"What for?"

"I have some good news. Turn that off and come over and sit down."

Jonah huffed out an irritated sigh. "I was almost to the next level."

Sara studied his face a moment, her emotions churning in an odd mixture of love and apprehension. "I got a job today. A very good one. It'll mean we can do all kinds of fun things in the future. We can take trips and explore."

Jonah frowned. "What kind of job? Where is it?"

"It's a job like I had at Crowley's, only better. It's in San Francisco."

"Where's that?"

"California. There's so much to do there. You'll love it."

"No, I won't. I like it here." Jonah crossed his arms over his chest and flopped back against the couch.

A sour knot swirled in her stomach. "I know you do, but this was only temporary. You knew that. Now it's time to go and be our own family again."

"I like this family. I have a cousin, and there's a dog to play with, and I can do what I want and play on a team, and I like my school." He gave her an icy glare. "I'm not leaving."

Sara inhaled sharply. Her son had never back-talked her, ever. She hadn't expected him to take the news well, but neither had she expected this reaction. "Jonah, I know this isn't what you wanted, but we'll come back and see the family. We can…" She touched her fingers to his slender shoulder, only to have him jerk away.

"I don't want to come back. I want to stay here forever. You go to the new job. I'm not leaving. I hate you."

Sara gasped. "Jonah."

"Leave me alone." He swiped angry tears from his face.

Jonah ran from the room, and she heard his bedroom door slam shut. She started after him, then stopped. She'd give him some time to calm down. Then they'd talk again. In time he would understand the move was for the best.

Back in her room she looked at her reflection in the mirror. It was for the best. Wasn't it? It would be hard to leave Blessing. In the time she'd been here she'd become comfortable, even peaceful. Things she hadn't known in a long time.

A half hour later, Sara went to Jonah's door and listened. She didn't hear any crying. Maybe he was ready to talk. She tapped lightly. When he didn't answer on the second knock she stepped inside. The room was empty. She checked the closet and the adjoining bath, but there was no sign of him. Had he gone downstairs?

A twinge of concern touched her nerves. He wasn't downstairs. Or on the deck or on the front porch. Concern turned to alarm. A crash of thunder rattled the windows, and the sound of pouring rain pounded the roof. Was he out in this weather? Grabbing an umbrella, she made a mad dash to the few outbuildings, but Jonah wasn't in any of them.

Fear closed off her throat. Her pulse refused to beat for a full second. Where was he? Would he run away from home? She had to find him. Back in the kitchen she pulled out her phone and started to call Camille, only to realize there was nothing she could do from the hospital. Whom could she call for help?

Luke.

She placed the call, hoping he would answer. They hadn't parted on good terms.

The sound of his voice gave her comfort. "Luke, I need your help. I can't find Jonah and…" Another boom of thunder shook the house. "I'm afraid he's out in this storm. I have to find him."

"We will. Tell me what happened?"

Sara filled him in quickly. "I knew he wouldn't want to leave Blessing, but I never dreamed he'd be so angry that he'd run away. I've searched everywhere. Where could he have gone?"

"I might have an idea. Let me check around."

"I'm coming over."

"No. You need to stay at the house in case he shows up. I promise I'll let you know the minute I find him."

"Luke, he's my baby."

"I know, sweetheart. Don't worry. I'll find him."

Sara clutched the phone in her hand, finding reassurance knowing Luke was there when she needed him. Moving to the back door she stared out the window and prayed that her son would be all right.

Chapter Twelve

Luke grabbed a jacket and pulled the hood over his head. He had a fairly good idea he'd find Jonah in the clubhouse he and Rusty had set up. It was the kind of place Luke would have gone to in the same situation. He prayed the boy was there, because if not he wasn't sure where else to look.

In the back of his mind the thought kept surfacing that Sara had taken a job in San Francisco. His chest tightened at the idea of her being so far away. He shouldn't be surprised but he'd hoped. It didn't matter what he'd hoped. Sara had made her decision.

The rainfall slackened as he neared the shed. A faint light shone through the small window. He knew the boys had collected several flashlights for their adventures. He didn't bother to knock. He pushed open the door and ducked inside. Jonah was huddled on one of the lounge chairs they'd rescued from the junk pile. Luke took a seat in one of the plastic chairs and waited.

Jonah stared at him, then hunkered down further, arms crossed protectively around his body. They sat in silence. Jonah finally spoke.

"What are you doing here?"

"Looking for you. Your mom was worried."

"Don't care. I hate her."

"Want to tell me what happened that made you hate her?"

"No. And I'm not going back. I'm going to live here in the clubhouse."

Luke glanced around the small shed. "Well, I can see why you would want to. It's pretty sweet here."

Jonah frowned. "She's making me move away from here and leave Rusty and Daisy and everything."

The pitiful tone in the boy's voice squeezed Luke's heart. "That's tough. But you know you'll always be cousins. You'll come back and visit."

"Will you be here?"

Luke thought about the real estate sign at the end of his drive. "I don't know."

"Then it won't be the same. I don't want things to change. I want it to stay the same. Why does she have to take a stupid job?"

"She wants to provide a good life for you. She needs a job to do that."

"She has a job at the store."

Luke wasn't sure how much the boy understood about his mother's situation, so he searched for a way to explain. "Do you know that your mom doesn't get paid for working at the store?"

The boy frowned. "But she works there all the time."

"She is doing that to help your Aunt Camille. They made a pact. Like you and Rusty did when you started work on this clubhouse. You and your mom would live here for free, and in exchange, your mom agreed to fix up the store."

"She's working for free?"

Luke nodded. He could see the boy was mulling this information over. "It's called room and board. A place to live in exchange for work."

"That's dumb."

"Not really, but your mom agreed because she loves her sister, and she needed a home for you until she could find a new job. Your mom loves you, Jonah, very much, and she wants the best for you."

"Being here is best."

"Maybe. But there might be another place that's even better. But you'll never know if you run away. Change is hard for everyone. But it forces us to move forward, usually toward something better." Luke studied him a moment to see if he was getting through. "But because it's unknown, it's scary, so we want to stay where we are. We're afraid we might not like a new place or that we might not make any friends or we'll hate our school."

Jonah's lip quivered and he nodded. Luke reached over and laid a hand on his knee. "Coming here to Blessing was good. You found Rusty, and your aunt and uncle, lots of things you enjoyed. There could be even more happy surprises in your new home."

"Is that why you're leaving? To find a better place?"

Caught by his own advice, Luke saw the truth like a punch to the chest. He wasn't any smarter than this young boy. In his own way, Luke was running away, too. Sara saw it, but he'd been too blinded by the old fear to see clearly.

"I'm not sure, Jonah. I think we both have some hard thinking to do."

"Would you come and visit me if we move?"

Luke's throat tightened. In a heartbeat. But it

was a promise he couldn't keep. "I don't know, Jonah. But we can keep in touch."

Luke's phone rang, and he glanced at the screen. Sara. "It's your mom. I need to let her know you're okay." Jonah shrugged.

"Please tell me Jonah is with you."

"He's right here. We're in the clubhouse having a man-to-man discussion. No girls allowed."

Sara's voice cracked. "Thank the Lord. I'll be right there."

"Sorry, no girls allowed, but we're heading back soon." He looked at Jonah, who gave him a nod. Luke gave the boy a hug, a strange longing filling his chest. He'd like to be a dad to Sara's son. But he doubted he'd get the opportunity.

The rain had slowed to a light mist when they left the shed. The only sound was the dripping of drops from the leaves as they made their way through the tree line.

Sara was standing on the back deck silhouetted by the porch light when they stepped through the wooded path onto the grassy yard. Even from several yards away he could see the tension in her body.

Luke touched the boy's shoulder. "Go on. She's waiting for you. And Jonah, remember. She was scared, so be kind."

Jonah took off at a trot and received a big hug when he reached his mother. Luke quickly turned and walked back into the sheltered woods. Sara's world was complete. Now he had to see to his own.

Sara rearranged the collection of mercury glass on the buffet table for the fourth time. Her concentration today was absent. Her mind was still on last night and Jonah's response to the news of her new job in San Francisco. She pressed her fingers to her throat. The ache inside still gnawed at her. She never imagined her son would react by running away. The terror she'd endured during that time was something she never wanted to experience ever again.

Taking a step back, she studied the arrangement again. Useless. Maybe Alice could do a better job. Sara had talked with Jonah for a long time last night, trying to make him understand, but it had little effect on his desire to remain in Blessing. She hadn't told him, but she wasn't ready to leave the small town, either. She'd found a sense of contentment and satisfaction here with the store and her family.

Why couldn't she have found a job in New Orleans or Nashville? Those cities were at least within easy driving distance to Blessing. She had promised Jonah they would visit often. The idea of living so far from her sister wasn't as appealing as it had once been. They'd grown close, and it felt good to be near family.

Sara walked to the kitchen and poured another cup of coffee. Maybe the caffeine would jump-start her creativity. The back door opened, and Luke stepped inside. The sight of his tall, lean frame and his handsome face sent trickles of warmth along her nerves. She smiled. "Good morning."

He held her gaze a long moment. "Hi. I, uh, wanted to see how you were doing this morning. And Jonah, too."

Sara welcomed the opportunity to talk things over with Luke. "Care for a cup of coffee?"

"Always."

They settled at the small table in the corner of the kitchen. "I'm glad you stopped by. I wanted to thank you for your help last night. Knowing you were looking for Jonah kept me from going mad with worry."

"I'm happy I was there to help. I was worried, too. I'm glad I found him at the first place I looked."

"I guess I'll have to visit that clubhouse he

loves so much." Her heart skipped a beat when she remembered that she wouldn't be here much longer. Her life was moving on.

Luke pointed a finger at her. "No can do. No girls allowed, remember?"

She smiled, then took a sip of her coffee. "Jonah told me what you said to him. I appreciate you having my back. I know this job isn't a popular decision, but it was necessary."

Luke nodded. "I really do understand, Sara. Congrats on the job. I hope it's everything you wanted."

She held his gaze a moment, memorizing his blue eyes and the different flecks of gold and gray in his irises. Her memories had suddenly become very important. One memory needed to be corrected. "Luke, I want to apologize for the things I said to you the other night. I was out of line. You have the right to your feelings. I shouldn't have dismissed them."

Luke laid his hand on hers. "Don't be. You gave me a lot to think about."

Her hopes took flight. "Are you changing your mind about leaving?"

He withdrew his hand and leaned back. "No."

Sara swallowed her disappointment. After

all, she wouldn't be here, either. "Any nibbles on the farm?"

"Not yet. Apparently no one wants a hundred acres, a barn workshop and a house that needs a complete restoration."

An awkward silence formed between them. There was so much she wanted to say, but the timing was never right. What would he say if she told him she loved him? Would it change anything?

Luke tapped the side of his cup with his finger. "When do you have to be on the job?"

She didn't want to talk about that now. "Soon. What happens if the farm won't sell?"

"I'll go anyway. I don't have to be here to sell it. Jonah asked me to visit him in San Francisco. I told him I couldn't, but that we could keep in touch—if that's all right."

"Of course. He adores you. He talks about you all the time. He told me once he wished you were his dad." Heat flooded her cheeks. The thoughts that filled her mind were not appropriate now.

"I wouldn't mind having him as a son, either."

The air in her lungs stilled, making it hard to breathe. She held his gaze, wishing there were words to make everything right between them. Wanting to find a way to keep them here in Blessing and close together.

Her heart was crying out, and she could tell Luke was struggling, too. "Thank you. That means a lot. *You* mean a lot. If things had worked out differently, we might have…" She bit her lip. "I guess we both have a new road to travel."

"I suppose so." He stood and moved toward the door, then turned back. His eyes were piercing and intense. "Fred told me it was time I declared myself."

"What do you mean?"

He came to her and pulled her up in front of him, the palm of one hand caressing her cheek. She swayed toward him, anticipating what was to come. He kissed her, leaving no doubt whatsoever of his feelings and siphoning all her strength in the process. He ended the kiss and held her close, speaking softly into her ear.

"Sara, I love you. I think I have since you looked so embarrassed that first day when you learned the surprise was baked goods. I don't want to be in Blessing if you're not here."

Tears stung her eyes. Why was their timing always so lousy? "I have to go. I have to take care of Jonah."

"I agree. He should always come first."

Sara gazed into his eyes, her emotions in turmoil. "Luke, I love you, too. It's just that…"

Luke pulled her close and kissed her again. The kiss was soft, tender and brief. A kiss that said goodbye. Her chest compressed with the pressure of an anvil.

Luke walked through the door, and Sara had the sick feeling she would never see him again.

Sara retreated to the small office and closed the door. If only she could close the door on her emotions as easily. She couldn't hide here forever. Her path was clear. The door had been opened to her new life. Picking up her cell phone, she dialed. Time to formally accept the job.

"I'm so sorry, Mrs. Holden, but we filled that position early this morning. We were hoping to hear from you sooner. Another suitable candidate was found."

Every molecule in Sara's body turned to ice. No. This couldn't be happening. How had she made such a big mistake? What was she supposed to do now?

She looked up as Alice peeked in. "You want to come look at that mercury glass display? I found some old dresser scarves—what's wrong? What's happened?"

Sara didn't bother to fight the tears coming down her cheeks. "I lost the job."

"What? How? I thought it was a done deal."

"I messed up. They told me they needed an answer soon, but I got so caught up in Jonah last night and then this morning Luke came by, and by the time I called them back they'd found somebody else."

Alice handed her a tissue. "That's awful. I'm so sorry. What are you going to do?"

A sarcastic laugh escaped her throat. "Oh, you know what they say. When God closes a door, He opens a window."

"Does He really?" Alice perched on the edge of the desk. "Does God close a door, or do we do it ourselves and blame Him?"

"What do you mean?"

"Well, what if we are the one who closes it because we don't want to change or because we want to make sure our plans and dreams are going in the right direction? The open window is just a way to rationalize our control."

Sara was too upset to mull over Alice's comment. She had to tell Camille that she'd lost her golden opportunity. She'd be needing her sister's support a while longer. At least Jonah would be happy. And there was that job in

Maine that was still open. Though that was a last resort.

"I'm not feeling well. I'm going home. Will you be all right today without me?"

Alice gave her a quick hug. "Yes. Go. Take some time to get things sorted. Call if you need me for anything."

Sara never intended to drive to the Blessing Bridge but found herself pulling into the parking lot. The peaceful grounds beckoned her. Slowly, she strolled down the pathway that wound through the flowers and trees to the old arched bridge.

She stopped at the pinnacle of the bridge, her gaze drifting over the serene landscape. It was the middle of October and the trees were still green and the weather balmy. She liked that about Blessing. Truthfully, there was so much she liked here. She liked the people. She liked being near her sister. She liked how the store had turned out. She liked seeing Jonah happy and confident. She liked Luke. No. She loved Luke.

That had not been in her plan. Ever. But there it was. He loved her, too, but not enough to risk any kind of relationship.

She'd made a mess of her life. Jonah was unhappy, Luke was out of her life, she was unemployed and with little hope now of another position opening up. For the first time in her life, she was lost. She had no future, no plan, no path, no direction. She'd always been in control of her life, and now she couldn't control anything anymore. Not even her own emotions. And try as she might, she could see no way out of her dilemma.

Camille was fond of referencing the verse about the Lord working all things for good, but she couldn't see how anything good could be pulled from this mess. Tears flowed again. She hated crying. It accomplished nothing.

Sara closed her eyes and opened her palms. "Lord, please help me. I don't know what to do or where to turn. I thought I understood what You wanted me to do, but You shut that door and now I'm lost."

She opened her eyes. She'd hoped to find some direction here in the park. Some insight, a thought or flicker of an idea about what to do next. She closed her eyes. Another plan that had failed.

As she gazed out at the lush grounds in front of her, she thought back and realized that despite her efforts and determination, few of her plans had actually worked out. She was constantly adjusting and rearranging, trying to keep things moving forward.

Alice's comment came to mind. Had she subconsciously sabotaged her own plan? Had God been closing doors, or had she been forcing her ideas into situations? Her plans. Her ideas of what should take place. Maybe it was time to let go and see what the Lord's plan for her might be.

Would His plan include Luke? Luke had accused her of running from her past, afraid to risk her heart again. Was she? Was she afraid of loving Luke because of her history with relationships?

Luke was nothing like her dad or Elliot. She should never have compared him to them. Her gaze scanned the park again as she strolled slowly back to her car. Evidence of Luke's character was on display here for all to see. The benches he'd crafted so skillfully and donated, each carrying a Bible verse. His faith was evident in everything he did. Where was her faith? Would anyone know she was a believer just by being around her?

Her phone rang, and she hesitated to answer. She had some soul searching to do. She glanced at the screen. Camille. Maybe something was wrong. "Hey, sis. Everything okay?"

"Yes. We're all fine, but I would like you to come to the hospital. I want to talk to you."

The odd tone in her sister's voice made her uneasy and the drive to the hospital feel twice as long.

Something was wrong. Maybe she and Jonah had outstayed their welcome. Having boarders, even family, put a strain on any relationship. On the other hand, she couldn't imagine Camille tossing them out on their ears. That went against her caring nature.

But why else would her sister summon her to the hospital?

Sara's nerves were on edge when she entered her sister's hospital room. During the ride here she'd had plenty of time to imagine all kinds of scary reasons her sister wanted to talk. Dave was sitting beside the bed holding Camille's hand. She looked between them. Neither one seemed upset. "What's happened? Are the babies all right?"

Camille chuckled softly. "Yes, of course. We're coming home tomorrow. We just wanted to talk to you about something."

Sara exhaled and sank into the other chair. "Oh. Well, before you start, I have to tell you that my job fell through. I took too long to respond, so Jonah and I might have to stay here a little longer. I hope that's okay."

Husband and wife exchanged glances and then smiled. "Of course, sis. In fact, that will work out perfectly."

"For what?"

"Sis, I've come to realize that I'm not really interested in running the store. Since the twins have arrived I don't want to leave them for a second. I want to stay home with them." The couple exchanged looks. "Which means I need someone to manage the store. I was hoping you'd stay and take charge. I'm not really cut out to be a businesswoman like you. Everyone in town has told me what a wonderful job you've done. I'm so grateful. I can never repay you for all your help."

Sara hadn't expected this turn of events. "Are you serious? About me taking over?"

"Actually, I'd like for you to buy me out. I know there's a lot to work through, but please, say you'll stay here in Blessing and help me out."

Like the sun rising over the horizon, Sara saw her future. One she'd never dreamed possible. The answer to her life. A plan the Lord had devised that was perfect for her. And Luke.

"Yes. Yes, I will. Thank you. You've answered my prayer. But I have to go. I have to get back to Blessing."

She moved to her sister and gave her a hug. "You have no idea what you've done."

"Good, I hope."

"Very, very good, but I still have to convince someone else to get on board."

"Luke?"

Sara nodded.

"I'm not worried. He's perfect for you. Go. Catch yourself a carpenter."

Camille might not be worried but Sara was. The ride back to Blessing gave her plenty of time to come up with a plan. One she earnestly offered up in prayer. If her plan didn't work, then she'd wait and see what the Lord's plan would produce, but she had a feeling she had it right this time.

The more she thought about Camille's offer the more excited she became. Running the New Again was a perfect solution. Decorating was her happy place. It was where she felt she belonged. It was where she fit. She fit with Luke, too. They belonged together. She'd never imagined that she would find fulfillment with a handsome carpenter, a farm in a small Southern town and a business all her own.

God really did make all things work for good. All we had to do was get out of His way.

All she had to do now was confront Luke. And she wasn't taking no for an answer.

Luke sat on his front porch steps later that afternoon staring down the tree-lined driveway. It was one of the reasons he'd bought the house. Each time he pulled onto the property he thanked the Lord for the row of stately live oaks that welcomed him home.

He'd miss that. He'd miss the sight of the large barn where he worked, the old silo in the distance and the tree line between his property and the Atkinses'. That narrow path connected him to Sara and Jonah. He'd miss that, too. He wasn't sure how he'd cope with them gone. The lack of interested buyers in his farm meant he might have to linger in Blessing longer than he'd planned. It didn't feel right to leave and let the real estate agent handle things.

Luke glanced up at the sound of a car approaching between the trees. Sara's car appeared. She pulled to a stop at the edge of his lawn and got out. She was holding the small red For Sale topper from the real estate sign at the road.

He stood as she hurried toward him. There

was an odd light in her eyes and an unusual smirk on her lips.

She stopped in front of him, close enough for him to catch a hint of her perfume. He steeled himself.

"Hi."

She was breathless when she spoke. Was something wrong? "Hello. I thought you'd be home packing for the big move."

She waved off his comment. "Oh that. I lost that job."

His chest tightened. Another of her plans shattered. She must be devastated, but she didn't act like it. "I'm sorry."

She shook her head. "Don't be." She smiled up at him. "I have a new plan. Want to hear it?"

"Sure. I guess." He couldn't imagine what she'd come up with.

Sara took the sign, bent it in half and tossed it over her shoulder. "You don't need to sell the farm, because we're staying put."

"We are?"

"Yes. I don't want to take Jonah away from his cousin or his family or you or Daisy." She took a step closer. "And I don't want to go, either. I like the South. It's warm all the time. I really like Blessing. It feels like home."

Her nearness was playing havoc with his

emotions. All he wanted to do was take her in his arms and kiss her senseless. "What about all those plans for Jonah and the big-city advantages?"

"I've discovered there are greater advantages here. For both of us."

Sara took hold of his hand. "Luke, I love you. I have for a while, but I was too afraid to admit it. You were right. I was hiding from my emotions out of fear. I didn't think I'd ever find a man I could trust, but I did. You. And I thought I'd lost everything, you, my job, a future, but then I gave all my plans over to the Lord and He worked it out. Perfectly. All I had to do was step aside and let Him work."

"What worked out? You're not making any sense."

She laughed. "Everything has changed, and it all fell into place. Camille wants me to take over the store. She wants to stay home with the twins. I'll be able to help with the babies, and Jonah can stay in his school and be near his cousin."

"And why does this mean I don't have to sell the farm?" She looked at him as if he were dense.

"Don't you see? I'll be running New Again, perhaps owning it in the future, and you can build your furniture which we'll sell in the store. It's perfect for both of us. We get to do what we love and be…together."

Her smile faded, and her eyes filled with doubt. "That is if you want to be together. Please, Luke, don't let me leave."

Luke struggled to grasp the sudden change. Sara loved him. She wasn't leaving, and she wanted to be together. "Are you sure?"

"Yes. For the first time in my life, I know where I belong. With you. We can put all the doubts and fears and shadows of our pasts behind us because I know that, together, we can overcome anything."

"You think so?" He touched her cheek. "What makes you so sure?"

"Because we belong together. Forever."

"Are you asking me to marry you?" He took hold of her shoulders.

"Would you? If I asked you nicely."

He shrugged. "Let me think about it."

Sara grasped his shirt in her fingers. "Luke?"

He pulled her into his arms and kissed her with all the promise he had for the future. A life with Sara was all he needed. He ended the kiss, breathless and flushed. "Yes. I'll marry you. On one condition."

She frowned. "You're not going to reveal another secret, are you?"

Luke chuckled. "No. Secrets are not allowed from here on. I want you to help me restore this old hulk of a house."

She threw her arms around his neck. "Yes. I fell in love with the house the moment I stepped inside. It felt like home. *You* feel like home."

Luke held her close, finding in Sara's embrace the peace he'd been searching for.

She raised her head, her eyes filled with love. "We need to tell Jonah."

He nodded. "How do you think he'll take the news of us being together?"

"He'll be overjoyed. Remember, I told you he mentioned once he'd like to have you for his father."

"It's a big responsibility."

She grinned. "But that's not all. He told me he wants a dog of his own."

Luke nodded. "We can make that happen."

She touched his chest lightly. "And he would like to have a baby brother like his cousin has."

Luke's heart raced, beating in time with Sara's. "We can make that happen, too."

Sara wrapped her arms around his neck, holding him tightly. "Or a sister."

Luke chuckled. "As long as we're together, nothing else matters."

Luke sent up a prayer of gratitude. His life was finally complete. Sara had not only revitalized the store, but she'd come into his life and made it new again.

Luke took her hand. "Let's go tell Jonah."

They walked together to the path between the trees that now linked them to their family and their future.

* * * * *

Dear Reader,

I hope you've enjoyed Luke and Sara's journey to their happily-ever-after. Overcoming a traumatic event in our lives isn't easy. When you've been scarred, the tissue takes a long time to heal, and the emotions connected with it live near the surface. Luke and Sara each had life-changing events to overcome. Writing their journey has been a challenge but a satisfying one. They needed each other and their faith to push through the old fears, and find freedom and love with each other. You may not have a Blessing Bridge to go to, but you have access to the Lord at all times. Whatever your obstacle, keep forging ahead. Our trials have to be gone through, not around. I love to hear from readers. You can follow me on Twitter, @lorrainebeatty, or Facebook at Lorraine Beatty Author.

Blessings,
Lorraine

Author's Note

The inspiration for Luke's special rocking chair came from a local Mississippi crafts-man. Greg Harkins is known as the Rocking Chair Man. Harkins designs each rocker to be unique and has provided rocking chairs for six presidents, many celebrities and a pope. I don't know if Luke's chairs will achieve the same notoriety, but it's fun to think about.

Get 4 FREE REWARDS!

We'll send you 2 FREE Books plus 2 FREE Mystery Gifts.

FREE
Value Over
$20

Both the **Harlequin® Special Edition** and **Harlequin® Heartwarming™** series feature compelling novels filled with stories of love and strength where the bonds of friendship, family and community unite.

YES! Please send me 2 FREE novels from the Harlequin Special Edition or Harlequin Heartwarming series and my 2 FREE gifts (gifts are worth about $10 retail). After receiving them, if I don't wish to receive any more books, I can return the shipping statement marked "cancel." If I don't cancel, I will receive 6 brand-new Harlequin Special Edition books every month and be billed just $5.49 each in the U.S. or $6.24 each in Canada, a savings of at least 12% off the cover price, or 4 brand-new Harlequin Heartwarming Larger-Print books every month and be billed just $6.24 each in the U.S. or $6.74 each in Canada, a savings of at least 19% off the cover price. It's quite a bargain! Shipping and handling is just 50¢ per book in the U.S. and $1.25 per book in Canada.* I understand that accepting the 2 free books and gifts places me under no obligation to buy anything. I can always return a shipment and cancel at any time by calling the number below. The free books and gifts are mine to keep no matter what I decide.

Choose one: ☐ **Harlequin Special Edition** ☐ **Harlequin Heartwarming**
(235/335 HDN GRJV) **Larger-Print**
(161/361 HDN GRJV)

Name (please print)

Address   Apt. #

City   State/Province   Zip/Postal Code

Email: Please check this box ☐ if you would like to receive newsletters and promotional emails from Harlequin Enterprises ULC and its affiliates. You can unsubscribe anytime.

Mail to the Harlequin Reader Service:
IN U.S.A.: P.O. Box 1341, Buffalo, NY 14240-8531
IN CANADA: P.O. Box 603, Fort Erie, Ontario L2A 5X3

Want to try 2 free books from another series? Call 1-800-873-8635 or visit www.ReaderService.com.

*Terms and prices subject to change without notice. Prices do not include sales taxes, which will be charged (if applicable) based on your state or country of residence. Canadian residents will be charged applicable taxes. Offer not valid in Quebec. This offer is limited to one order per household. Books received may not be as shown. Not valid for current subscribers to the Harlequin Special Edition or Harlequin Heartwarming series. All orders subject to approval. Credit or debit balances in a customer's account(s) may be offset by any other outstanding balance owed by or to the customer. Please allow 4 to 6 weeks for delivery. Offer available while quantities last.

Your Privacy—Your information is being collected by Harlequin Enterprises ULC, operating as Harlequin Reader Service. For a complete summary of the information we collect, how we use this information and to whom it is disclosed, please visit our privacy notice located at corporate.harlequin.com/privacy-notice. From time to time we may also exchange your personal information with reputable third parties. If you wish to opt out of this sharing of your personal information, please visit readerservice.com/consumerschoice or call 1-800-873-8635. **Notice to California Residents**—Under California law, you have specific rights to control and access your data. For more information on these rights and how to exercise them, visit corporate.harlequin.com/california-privacy.

HSEHW22R3

THE 2022 LOVE INSPIRED CHRISTMAS COLLECTION

Buy 3 and get 1 FREE!

May all that is beautiful, meaningful and brings you joy be yours this holiday season...including this fun-filled collection featuring 24 Christmas stories. From tender holiday romances to Christmas Eve suspense, this collection has it all.

YES! Please send me the **2022 LOVE INSPIRED CHRISTMAS COLLECTION** in Larger Print! This collection begins with ONE FREE book and 2 FREE gifts in the first shipment. Along with my FREE book, I'll get another 3 Larger Print books! If I do not cancel, I will continue to receive four books a month for five more months. Each shipment will contain another FREE gift. I'll pay just $23.97 U.S./$26.97 CAN., plus $1.99 U.S./$4.99 CAN. for shipping and handling per shipment.* I understand that accepting the free books and gifts places me under no obligation to buy anything. I can always return a shipment and cancel at any time. My free books and gifts are mine to keep no matter what I decide.

☐ 298 HCK 0958   ☐ 498 HCK 0958

Name (please print)

Address   Apt. #

City   State/Province   Zip/Postal Code

> **Mail to the Harlequin Reader Service:**
> **IN U.S.A.:** P.O. Box 1341, Buffalo, NY 14240-8531
> **IN CANADA:** P.O. Box 603, Fort Erie, ON L2A 5X3
